CASE FILES

UNS LVED

Crime And Punishment

Edited By Debbie Killingworth

First published in Great Britain in 2021 by:

 Young**Writers**® — Est. 1991 —

Young Writers
Remus House
Coltsfoot Drive
Peterborough
PE2 9BF
Telephone: 01733 890066
Website: www.youngwriters.co.uk

Printed and bound in the UK by BookPrintingUK
Website: www.bookprintinguk.com
YB0479I

FOREWORD

As long as there have been people, there has been crime, and as long as there have been people, there have also been stories. Crime fiction has a long history and remains a consistent best-seller to this day. It was for this reason that we decided to delve into the murky underworld of criminals and their misdeeds for our newest writing competition.

We challenged secondary school students to craft a story in just 100 words on the theme of 'Unsolved'. They were encouraged to consider all elements of crime and mystery stories: the crime itself, the victim, the suspect, the investigators, the judge and jury. The result is a variety of styles and narrations, from the smallest misdemeanors to the most heinous of crimes. Will the victims get justice or will the suspects get away with murder? There's only one way to find out!

Here at Young Writers it's our aim to inspire the next generation and instill in them a love of creative writing, and what better way than to see their work in print? The imagination and flair on show in these stories is proof that we might just be achieving that aim! The characters within these pages may have to prove their innocence, but these authors have already proved their skill at writing!

CONTENTS

Andalusia Academy Primary School, St Matthias Park

Jihaan Ali (13)   1
Fardowza Omar (15)   2
Ayse Turkmen (13)   3
Zayna Al-Sakkaf (12)   4
Sarah Khan (13)   5

Budehaven Community School, Bude

Niamh Collen (13)   6
Will Robins (16)   7
Katie Ashley (14)   8
Connie Copplestone (14)   9
Charlotte Conway (12)   10
Seren Stafford (12)   11
Lexi-Rose Sargent (11)   12
Jess Lewin (13)   13

Greenford High School, Southall

Shri Pankhania (13)   14
Ella Watts (13)   15
Mohemmed Shakeel (13)   16
Yaameen Githroo (13)   17
Kiran Bhachu (13)   18
Steven Carvalho Da Silva (13)   19
Tej Vendikantham (13)   20
Hangama Hesari (13)   21
Samira Dirir (12)   22
Rhythm Sharma (13)   23
Raagni Pallan (13)   24
Assena Sadiqi (13)   25
Adam Yousaf (13)   26

Sariah Mudhar (13)   27
Dyari Saeed (13)   28
Shrey Patel (11)   29
Daniel Kay (13)   30
Abdulqader Bakhshi (13)   31
Dina Alttaief (13)   32
Elvira Zbigli (13)   33
Jaspreet Souni (11)   34
Leeya Gill (11)   35
Amirah Mire (13)   36
Ashmidha Sivakangan (13)   37
Shakira Cybulska-Iynkaran (11)   38
Sayuri Mistry (12)   39
Alex Bizazinski (12)   40
Olivia Galik (12)   41
Noor Khalil (12)   42
Ghazal Hakimi (13)   43
Haris Sayanthan (13)   44

Stoneygate School, Great Glen

Bradley Mushambi (14)   45
Lauren Wong (14)   46
Oliver Cadby-Lynch (12)   47
Skylar Gill (14)   48
Harry Surtees (14)   49
Josh Martin Sweeney (13)   50
Aryan Aziz (13)   51
Mia van Leeuwen (11)   52

The Willink School, Burghfield Common

Ludmila Kobiera (12)	53
Taylor Robinson (13)	54
Sophie Jubb (13)	55
Charlie Chapman (12)	56
Nathan Audsley (13)	57
Ewan Morgan (12)	58
Molly Yeardley (13)	59
Samuel Lambourne (13)	60
Beth Cook (13)	61
Holly Brown (13)	62
Devon Baggs (13)	63
Freddy Durrant (12)	64
Ollie Sebright (13)	65
Arthur Harvey (12)	66
Jasmine Turner (13)	67
Kai McKenna (13)	68
LuisJohn Alexander (13)	69
Ava Standen (13)	70
Michele Bros (13)	71
Rahul Thomas (13)	72
Alexander Lee (13)	73
Jon-Lee Cole (13)	74
Grace Uren (13)	75

Wyvern St Edmund's, Laverstock

Eva Burden (12)	76
Alice Johnson (12)	77
Lucy Reynolds (14)	78
Charlotte Sims (12)	79
Summer Pearce (14)	80
Charlotte Downer (13)	81
Emilie Reece (13)	82
Anabelle Bosworth (14)	83
Lizzie Bolton (12)	84
Isaac Wright (11)	85
Sofia Manicom (12)	86
Carla Carpenter-Paya (11)	87
Helena Peska (14)	88
Tarian Nix (12)	89
Alice Ewen Benns (14)	90

George Nash (13)	91
Alice Natelson-Carter (13)	92
Sienna Searle (14)	93
Ella-Louise McCartney (12)	94
Hannah Waterworth (14)	95
Sophie Ollivierre (14)	96
Laura Massie (14)	97
Molly Williams (14)	98
Oliver Leak (13)	99
Fern Shearer (12)	100
Stanley Maculewicz (11)	101
Jessica Teltow (13)	102
Grace Harwood (13)	103
Anita Biju (12)	104
Ben Millman (14)	105
Shelby Roxburgh (13)	106
Amy Marshall (12)	107
Ella Becker (11)	108
Fergus Sime (12)	109
Joseph Holme (12)	110
Bradley Stewart (12)	111
Olivia Harris (14)	112
Gabriella Manicom (12)	113
Kara Lyons (12)	114
Hannah Reader (14)	115
Jessica Jackson (13)	116
Isabelle Malata (12)	117
Amelia Weston (13)	118
Kaitlin Stewart (13)	119
Ethan Reeve (13)	120
Eleanor Ollivierre (13)	121
Coco Jones (14)	122
Niamh Ball (14)	123
Evan Tonkinson (11)	124
Eva Hammond (11)	125
Hetty Gray (13)	126
Olivia Glover (14)	127
Reuben Leinster (12)	128
Bethany Alford (13)	129
Prerna Magenni (12)	130
Jack Dewey (12)	131
Jasmine Halliwell (13)	132
William Pearce (12)	133

Molly Taylor-Rice (11)	134	Louis Knight (13)	177
Chloe Martin (13)	135	Catherine Hinder (14)	178
Poppy Partridge (13)	136	Casey Mullen (14)	179
Izabella Grand-Scrutton (12)	137	Ruby Goddard (12)	180
Miley Poulter (11)	138	George Chapman (12)	181
Daniel Hawkes (12)	139	Keira Crossen (14)	182
Elizabeth Lord (14)	140	Daisy Barney (14)	183
A Evans (13)	141	Matthew Osgood (12)	184
Maddie Coombes (12)	142	Sophie Everett (14)	185
Sydney Gape (14)	143	Alexia Roxburgh (12)	186
Eva Whittingham (11)	144		
Olivia Toms (14)	145		
Evelyn Lambert (13)	146		
Eloise (13)	147		
Jack Whyler (12)	148		
Chloe Guttridge (14)	149		
Lily Burt (12)	150		
Abby Azzopardi (12)	151		
Summer Wickham-Hughes (12)	152		
Grace Peter (14)	153		
Finn McCormack (12)	154		
Poppy Durham (12)	155		
Amelia Wells (14)	156		
Lekeisha Eletu (13)	157		
Lilli Clements-Champion (11)	158		
Bronte Pearce (12)	159		
Amelia Johns (12)	160		
Raneem Al Slamat (12)	161		
Amelia Moore (13)	162		
Freyda Nguyen-Vincent (13)	163		
Thomas James (13)	164		
Pippa-Mae Muirhead (11)	165		
Lizzie Bulpitt (14)	166		
Cassie Pearce (14)	167		
Bayley-James Jones (13)	168		
Abigail Hallen (13)	169		
Katie Dixon (13)	170		
Reuben Bowler (12)	171		
Zach Hiscott (12)	172		
Olivia Taylor (12)	173		
Zara Watson (12)	174		
Megan Lynn (12)	175		
Amelia Mullaney (14)	176		

THE STORIES

UNFAIR CIRCUMSTANCES

The cars blocked her path. Defeated, she got out of the vehicle, hands in the air. You could hear the police sirens from extremely far away, a girl was being handcuffed and led into a car. She could hear the police officers, from outside, muttering about how ruthless her crime was. It soon hit her she could end up in prison.

"He deserved it, he killed my mother."

"Where were you then?" the officer scoffed and led her out of the car. She was taken into a holding cell, hearing the officer muttering as he locked the door... "Disgusting."

Jihaan Ali (13)
Andalusia Academy Primary School, St Matthias Park

IDENTICAL

She was watching, she's consistently watching, sometimes I see shadows move while she's studying me, my replica. We are identical but inside I know something more sinister is at play. Leaving home in the morning she was shadowing me; out of sight, always. When I arrived, she was not present... I knew she was still there. As I turned into an alleyway, she was standing over the body of a bloody, battered man. At that moment, I realised. Police sirens rang in my ears. I was suddenly lying on the cold, hard ground, withering from the impact of the laser.

Fardowza Omar (15)
Andalusia Academy Primary School, St Matthias Park

BEHIND MY BACK

On my day off and I'm still doing work. I couldn't avoid this though, it was my uncle's corpse that was missing from his funeral. It was... original. Although, it was a pain that the guests and police had not found any evidence after searching for six hours. It was getting late so I headed home. The hot weather erupted a foul stench which introduced flies as I opened my window. I'd continue searching tomorrow. As I parked near the crime scene the next day, a guest screeched and pointed towards the inside of my boot.. At my deceased uncle.

Ayse Turkmen (13)
Andalusia Academy Primary School, St Matthias Park

FUR SUIT MASSACRE

Marcus had been walking home when a man in a fur suit had been following him. Terrified, he turned. The guy stabbed him in his abdomen. He stumbled into the alleyway and toppled to the ground. The furry man's eyes widened. Pieces of artificial fur from his suit fell off onto his eyes, hindering his sight. Marcus saw a chance. He tackled the man, still clenching the knife wound. He grabbed the mask and ripped it off with all his might, but something was wrong. The man... had no face! Just exposed flesh. Something strange was coming...

Zayna Al-Sakkaf (12)
Andalusia Academy Primary School, St Matthias Park

THE BLOODY DAGGER

One day, I came back from school and I was so exhausted, I decided to go straight to bed. After an hour or two of tranquil sleep, I was woken up by a screeching noise. I put on my black patterned slippers and rushed to see what it was. By the brunette fence, there was a dead body with blood oozing out of it and a greasy note. It read: 'Be warned! You're next'.

I was petrified and kept gawping at the door. Without me noticing, a tall figure entered my house and, *slash!* Instantly everything was covered in blood.

Sarah Khan (13)
Andalusia Academy Primary School, St Matthias Park

AMAYA'S FAULT

"She did it!" Adrien shouted as Mum walked in the room. He pointed his finger at the wall, exactly where he had just been doodling. "Amaya drew on the walls in my brand new pens!" he shouted. "Her fault!" Adrien blubbered to Mum, pointing at the broken frame. "It was Amaya, she punched the wall!" he smirked. "Amaya drowned my hamster!" he whimpered. "Amaya did it!" he accused. He always blamed me. "She did it Mum, Amaya did it!" He pointed to my lifeless body lying on the floor. It was like old times, though now the tears were real.

Niamh Collen (13)
Budehaven Community School, Bude

THE SPIDER TO THE FLY

"T'was meant to be a simple job; six ski masks, six loaded M8 assault rifles. Easy, efficient, effective! One of my donnys never turned up so we had to improvise, so a fly came along, that's what we call a new kid because the leader of the group aka 'the spider' is responsible to catch and kill the fly if they are caught ratting. I was the spider. When things went south, I went north, killed the kid... took the blame... and here we are!"
"Names?"
"Daniel, Max, Joshua, Sam, Jude."
"Thanks for ratting," said the spider to the fly.

Will Robins (16)
Budehaven Community School, Bude

FRAMED SUICIDE

Early one morning, I received an odd case. It was apparently attempted suicide but the thing that confused me was the teenage boy was afraid of cliffs and the sea. He had no psychological problems. Soon we dragged the drowned teen out of the large body of water. Forensic scientists examined the boy and found a startling discovery. There were other fingerprints on the body. We then suspected attempted murder. They soon started to search for suspects, checking the CCTV footage, pinpointing the murderer, placing them in prison. The fingerprints all matched up. But the prints were new...

Katie Ashley (14)
Budehaven Community School, Bude

LIFELESS

I heard something. It was a scream or smash. I couldn't tell over my heart racing. *Thump! Thump!* I didn't hear another sound. Maybe I should go check? No, I'll leave it. When I got there the next morning, it was too late. "Hello? Is anyone in?" I shouted. Silence. I headed in. Mess everywhere. Cracked photos lay on the floor. I made my way up the stairs, groaning at every step. Blood soaked into the carpet as the sun spilled in through the curtains. There she was, floating in cold, crimson water, eyes wide open. She was lifeless.

Connie Copplestone (14)
Budehaven Community School, Bude

THE BANK CAPTURE

I was on my way home from school. I was just passing the bank when I heard a smash. It was the bank's back window. Two men climbed out of the window. I slowly reached into my pocket and pulled out my phone so I could record the burglary. When the burglars noticed I was recording they started running towards me. I froze, stick-like, a popsicle. I had no idea what to do so I quickly stopped recording and screamed, "Help!" but no use. I kept screaming. No one noticed. Before I could yelp once more they reached me...

Charlotte Conway (12)
Budehaven Community School, Bude

THE RED MESSAGE

Forensics had dragged me back to the station again to review the ballistics results. When I finally returned home, it was to an eerie silence and then I realised my husband and daughter were gone. In the kitchen there was a message: 'Poison your boss if you want to see your family again. Oh and bring the superintendent's body'.

I shivered with shock as it now occurred to me that the crimson dripping finger paint on the cloud-white paper stuck to the fridge could be my child's blood...

Seren Stafford (12)

Budehaven Community School, Bude

SECRETS OF THE NIGHT

Once upon a time, in a land so close it was reachable by a five-minute walk, there lived a boy called Axel and a girl called Rhea. Axel was 17 and Rhea was 16. It was on one of their midnight walks that this story is set. A shrill female cry cut through the quiet midnight air, followed by three gunshots. Axel and Rhea stopped in their tracks and stared in the direction of the gunshots with looks of pleasure. They smiled. They laughed. All because they were in fact criminals, who arranged this murder.

Lexi-Rose Sargent (11)
Budehaven Community School, Bude

DEFINED BY DEATH

I really thought he loved me. All the plans we had made together, the future I had dreamed of. All a lie! So I did what needed to be done... I felt as though I was the one being punished. I didn't want to kill him, it wasn't my fault, but everything he had done to me was unforgivable. The body on the floor, the puddle of blood doesn't define me. A murderer I'm not. Someone in pain, yes. So with blood on my hands and knees, I stumbled to my feet, packed a bag and ran.

Jess Lewin (13)
Budehaven Community School, Bude

QUESTION AND ANSWER

"May I have this dance?" he whispered seductively.
I'll resist, taking my hips; I obliged. Trees stared like silent sentries. *Snap!* A twig ruptured from the ominous woods. Suddenly, pulling me in, we're a centimetre apart. "We're alone, correct?" I enquired. Dead silence. Antonis spun me gracefully, as I reeled in foreboding fog engulfed... "Argh!" My shrill scream rattled the forest like an earthquake. "Michael, you're supposed to be dead!"
Satan spun me: Antonis returned. A relief, I was probably deluded. Footsteps inched towards me. Something didn't add up.
"Raquel Smith, do the dead you killed, stay dead?" Antonis answered.

Shri Pankhania (13)
Greenford High School, Southall

1931

The year was 1931, and the air was cold. Summer nights were usually warm, but at this particular hour it was chilling. The streets were barren. Turning the keys and sliding open the heavy metal door attached to the car, a brunette emerged. The brunette immediately heard a gut-wrenching, crunching noise. He silently concluded his specific choice of parking was correct. While this period of contemplation commenced, the blonde making this noise had emerged from the shadows. "Ah! Detective William Soot!" The man with the cocoa-coloured curls spun swiftly on his heel. He immediately reached over for his gun. Oh no...

Ella Watts (13)
Greenford High School, Southall

DREAM

Screech! Screech! The boy's dream came true. It was amazingly real. Bats had entered the room, creating a really big chaos. The children were screaming and shouting. The loud erupting noises attracted the attention of neighbours. The kid went to the chicken shop every day after school. He once had a terrible dream that the chicken shop got destroyed and the next day it actually happened. His parents feared his disabilities and took him to several psychiatrists to get him 'fixed' but they all said, "Sorry, there's nothing we can do." The boy was depressed and devastated.

Mohemmed Shakeel (13)
Greenford High School, Southall

THE CASINO JOB

Masked men. Unknown getaway vehicle. Temporarily disabled cameras. Professional heist members. They managed to pull off a heist at the most lucrative casino in the city, nearly cleansing the gambling house of their ill-gotten gains and leaving with multiple duffle bags stuffed with millions of dollars in cash. Nothing was able to be traced, anyone on the property was quickly put down, judging on how swiftly the job was done, so no witnesses, only a massive crowd of after-party.

The perplexed cops aren't talking, nor are the disconsolate, depressed owners of the casino. Who and where are the suspects?

Yaameen Githroo (13)
Greenford High School, Southall

FRAMED

My lawyer stood beside me with an intrepid countenance for he knew that any sign of fear would land me in prison. Any moment now, my prosecutor would walk in. I only stole the money from his shop because I needed to pay my rent. Suddenly, a woman came rushing into the courtroom and whispered something into the judge's ear. The judge's face was immediately horrified. After a few minutes, he finally cleared his throat. He announced, "I am sorry to report that last night the prosecution was murdered." Loud murmurs filled the room. Everyone's eyes immediately fell on me...

Kiran Bhachu (13)
Greenford High School, Southall

THE STOLEN MONEY

It just didn't add up. How did they leave the bank with £10,000 billion? There were numerous armed police forces at the exit ready to fire and the bank only had one exit and one entrance. No secret tunnels and all the roads within a 100m radius were on lockdown. All the hostages were interrogated however all of them were found innocent. The whole bank had been searched professionally, however nothing was found, not even a single fingerprint. After days of interrogation and investigation, they couldn't find anything so the case was closed. What if they never left the bank?

Steven Carvalho Da Silva (13)
Greenford High School, Southall

AN IMPOSSIBLE MURDER

Surprised, the detective stayed wondering what happened. A dead body locked within a room with the murder weapon missing. Calmly, the detective glanced to the right, noticing a patch of velvet-red blood that was just about readable. It appeared to be a warning. The victim had tried to say something. Instantly, the detective realised this wasn't an ordinary murder. Suddenly, what sounded like a 1000 messages, came up. The detective was stunned and wondered if a gang could be behind this. That thought changed as soon as he saw a mysterious message in one of those 1000 messages...

Tej Vendikantham (13)
Greenford High School, Southall

THE LYING DETECTIVE

Mounted around the room, the marble statues had seen many people pass from their delicate displays to the next; now they watched someone pass away. Splattered a dark red, the room walls surrounded him in a crowded manner that seemed to make the space around him shrink. Beneath him, what used to be a vibrant Persian rug flowing with design began to absorb a new dye: his blood. Entering the room for the second time filled me with déjà vu, no guilt. My co-worker called me to the other side of the crime scene. "Detective, I think we've found something."

Hangama Hesari (13)
Greenford High School, Southall

A MASQUERADE OF DARKNESS

The orchestra of a thousand crickets echoed through the desolate city. Under silvery moonlight, destruction and rubble lay bare. Behind towering buildings tall metal bars were reaching for the dark, poisonous sky above; clouds stretched over the city like a dark cloak, moving swiftly and silently under the cover of the sky. A single shadow danced on the rooftops. It stopped dead in its tracks. Silhouettes swirled around him like a tornado. A velvet river of blood trickled down his ears. The soft thump of his heart slowed to a stop. No one knows who did it. A simple mystery.

Samira Dirir (12)
Greenford High School, Southall

I'M NOT GUILTY

"I didn't do it."
It was the second week in court. The same question over and over again. 'Did you kill your father?' They tortured me, the scars on my body each telling a different story. I sat in the corner of the chilled cell, why would they believe someone like me? I thought of the flashbacks of blood oozing out my wounds while my mother cried out, calling for help. Footsteps awoke me as a guard grabbed onto my wrist. Today was my 15th day here. The judge asked again, "Did you kill your father?"
"I didn't do it."

Rhythm Sharma (13)
Greenford High School, Southall

THE FINAL CLUE

Pages of notes strewn across the floor, she looked through each sentence with precision, reading it word for word far into the night. She matched three torn pieces together to form what looked like an address. The final clue? The woman hurried to her car. As she got closer and closer to the destination, she felt a sudden cloud of regret engulf her. She stepped out of the car cautiously and walked towards the strange silhouette that stood before her. She edged on the door and pushed it open, it was unlocked. There was nothing inside. The mystery remains unsolved.

Raagni Pallan (13)
Greenford High School, Southall

THE OTHER MOTHER

Sitting across me was a familiar face. She had my mother's eyes yet they were cold and lifeless. She had my mother's voice yet it was strained and ominous. Her movements seemed animated and her gestures forced. She looked like a doll with perfectly sewn seams, only they could be unravelled with one tug. She wore my mother's skin but it looked pale. I was about to reach over to feel her warmth when I heard her voice cry, "Stop!" But it wasn't strange like before and her lips hadn't moved. I then realised it was coming from behind me.

Assena Sadiqi (13)
Greenford High School, Southall

THE BERMUDA TRIANGLE

Crashing waves, violent storms and a triangle that encompasses it all. Missing boats, lost planes and drones that set out but never return. Berserk compasses and defective radars wash ashore the land of Florida and fade into history as if they were never there. It first appeared when Columbus set out to sea and ever since has been a sailor's unease. Only half a millennium later was it then recognised for its ferocity of hoarding all that set into its domain, with only a few escaping its grasp, living to tell the tale. Would you venture into the unknown?

Adam Yousaf (13)
Greenford High School, Southall

THE CONUNDRUM DOWNSTAIRS

I was certain everyone was asleep. Stealthily, I scampered towards the chamber permeated with gold and money that I had tried to pilfer. As I was engaged in my act, the corner of my eye perceived one of my fellow servants observing what I was doing. My jet-black pupils dilated. It would be the sixth servant I had to terminate. As I roamed the desolate, ghastly and hollow hallways I heard cries, screams and people gasping, last breaths coming from the basement. My face contorted into a peculiar plethora of shapes. If I was not murdering them, who was?

Sariah Mudhar (13)
Greenford High School, Southall

BETRAYED BY A BACKSTAB

I had an alibi, but of course they wouldn't believe me. I was betrayed. Everything around me is falling apart. I can't afford to be in this place. Convicts, criminals, culprits... and me. You see the odd one out in that list? Do you have any idea how this feels? The smell of perspiration and guilt flood my senses as I continue to rot alone in this cryptic cell. I'm to blame for ending up here. I've known him for ten years and I should've trusted my instincts a decade ago. Now I'm heading for the courtroom of death.

Dyari Saeed (13)
Greenford High School, Southall

THE HOSPITAL CRIME SCENE

I was in the hospital, waiting for my blood test results. The lights flickered. Everyone started screaming. I then saw a liquid substance that was departing from a body. I was terrified because an abundance of other people were dead too. *Was I going to be next?* I thought to myself. I started to run to the exit with five other people. We reached the door but it was locked. The flickering lights came back along with another pile of dead bodies. It was a pattern, when the flickering light came on a few people died. I shivered...

Shrey Patel (11)
Greenford High School, Southall

UNSOLVED

Thinking back, the witness must not have come forward. My last resort, and now I sit here, day 169... 169 missed chances of freedom, happiness and normality. All hope and faith lost. Then, I pace the room and ponder about how the police got the evidence? Someone must've set me up. But who? I have to think back more, you know what they say: 'Keep your friends close but your enemies closer'. I start frantically searching my mind for its prey. That brings me to two people I need to consider... Kevin and Nathan. Which one?

Daniel Kay (13)
Greenford High School, Southall

LAST MOMENTS

The lights turned on brightly, he sat in the chair. The man was surrounded by freshly painted walls, with one glass window. He then looked at his own reflection. It was the face of a killer. It was the face of a terrible monster. It was the face of a fully-fledged criminal. Suddenly a group of policemen entered the room in a single file. One of the policemen put a metal bowl on his head, which was attached to different coloured wires. Another of the policemen forcefully turned on a red switch. The death row inmate closed his eyes.

Abdulqader Bakhshi (13)

Greenford High School, Southall

UNSOLVED

The suspect was gone. We had absolutely no evidence whatsoever to restrain him. The poor innocent victim was silent as his whole life was reflected on. What could he have done so as not to be in this situation? His heart thumped. How was he going to gain justice for what he had been through and how had the suspect escaped the horrible crime he had committed. I felt sorrow and dismay. Everyone crowded around me to ensure that everything would be okay. I zoned out, all I could think about was the dreadful time I had been through.

Dina Alttaief (13)
Greenford High School, Southall

SENSELESS

A lifeless whisper resonated around the container. Unsure of whether I still wanted to know, my heart pounded in my chest and my stomach sank to my feet. I lay in the infinite darkness, numb and hollow. I felt an icy hand brush against my neck which startled me to my feet. I felt concrete for the first time when a deafening creak came from behind me. I tried to comprehend which one of my decisions landed me here. I was flooded with light until my head felt light and my eyes spun and unfocused. Sorry, that's all I remember.

Elvira Zbigli (13)
Greenford High School, Southall

THE UNSOLVED MYSTERY

Once again, winter had arrived. It was dark, late and misty outside. Dylan was asleep and her swift snoring was the reason I couldn't sleep. My eyes were wide open and I was staring out of the dusty window. For some reason, I thought the outside world was fascinating and different. All of a sudden, I realised that I was peering into the woods as a flash of light glinted under my eyes. Even though I wasn't allowed to at night, I tiptoed all the way to the front door. I slowly opened it to find just an empty forest...

Jaspreet Souni (11)
Greenford High School, Southall

RUN

Guilty I think? "Boo!" Run! I was scared. Pushing each tree out of my way as I ran through the forest. Someone was following me. I stopped to see if they were still there. I could see a shadow in the distance, so I carried on running. I stumbled upon a ditch and suspiciously looked inside. "Argh!" I fell in, I think I slipped or maybe I was pushed. I screamed and screamed for ages, but it was no use, no one would be able to hear me scream from all the way down there. I tried climbing my way up...

Leeya Gill (11)
Greenford High School, Southall

GUILT

'I know what you did...' My fingers trembled as I scanned the page over and over, not wanting to accept the words on the page. I glanced over at the locked door, a room that contained things that could lead me to my death. I decided to ignore the message, making my way to work. The familiar Scotland Yard sign came into view and I tapped my key card. The minute I entered guilt consumed me, knowing I was deceiving every one of my colleagues made me squirm. Yet I put a smile on my face and greeted them all.

Amirah Mire (13)
Greenford High School, Southall

UNSOLVED

Surging rapidly, the different hues of blood spilt onto the floor from the deep punctures in the victim's nape. The aroma of iron had wafted its way around the crime scene which had immensely possessed the detective's senses, he made his way to the body in a minute. Usually, he was indifferent and was very deceptive, but now the man staggered and twitched as he saw the dismembered body pinned to the headboard like a porcelain doll on display. Moving closer, he saw the succinct label... A gang symbol.

Ashmidha Sivakangan (13)
Greenford High School, Southall

UNSOLVED MYSTERY OF THE MISSING CHILDREN

It was a normal day in the town of Acronia, but something was odd, 'missing' posters filled the area and the missing people were all children. They were disappearing every two weeks, I knew this had to stop, but how? I'm only eleven but I guess I could have a go. I started off by trying to find clues. I walked around asking the missing children's parents where they'd gone before going missing, and when. They said the same thing, at the park at 15:40, so I went there but found nothing.

Shakira Cybulska-Iynkaran (11)
Greenford High School, Southall

THE BOX

Choked by its own overgrown branches, the forest resembled a sprawling fortress barricading the Earth from the warmth of the sun and the blue of the sky. I walked for what felt like days, red like paint stained my knees and elbows. I reached for my map, I was almost there. I huffed. As I walked the breeze tickled my arms, making the thrill of finding the box rush through every inch of my veins. Suddenly, out of the corner of my eye, I saw a dim light. I got closer and picked it up. I slowly opened it...

Sayuri Mistry (12)
Greenford High School, Southall

WHERE'S DANNY?

Mr Craige was a detective who worked for the police. He got a mysterious phone call at four in the morning. He picked up the phone and a strange voice from it spoke. "Hello, Jonathan Craige, I have your son trapped somewhere, where you can only find him from my clues. My first clue for you is that your son is in Hell's Kitchen and you have only ten minutes to get there..."
The call ended and Mr Craige was out of his seat frozen to the core at what he had just heard. What now?

Alex Bizazinski (12)
Greenford High School, Southall

DANGEROUS SAFEKEEPING

The van carried a wet stench of burnt carpets and boiled cabbage. A string of nausea slid through me as I glanced at the man's red eyes; I had never done anything like this before. But the memory of laughter when I had accepted his offer of a ride home kept me afloat. Soon I would be the one laughing. All I had to do was wait, wait for his realisation to hatch. The man had sent me out to get dinner and these humans were the easiest to catch.
Who am I? Why am I now killing the innocent?

Olivia Galik (12)
Greenford High School, Southall

THE KILLER MAZE

Icy fingers gripped my arm in the darkness as I heard somebody's footsteps. I ran rapidly into the fascinating maze but when I was inside the maze, I saw nothing but shadows around me so I decided to try and find a way out. I tried and tried but I was starting to lose hope. The clock which was on the spiky walls was ticking fast. As quickly as I could, I tried to figure out ways to get out of there and make it home before it was night-time, but I guess I was stuck there, panic-stricken.

Noor Khalil (12)
Greenford High School, Southall

THE UNSOLVED CASE

The lie detector results are back and as I suspected, they are all negative... The person that we have imprisoned for the time being was at the scene of the crime. There are multiple reports of illegal drug dealing in the area and we have to check it out immediately. Most of the suspects had run away by the time we got there and are now long lost, but one of the boys was caught and taken to the interrogation room which we are in right now. We need to keep trying to get the truth out of him.

Ghazal Hakimi (13)
Greenford High School, Southall

MYSTERY SHADOW

It was just a normal day at work for Babatunde, it was another crime but this was different. Many people had tried solving it but failed and were never seen again. But Babatunde was determined and had started to investigate the crime scene. He found a clue. Suddenly a gush of cold breeze swept by his cheeks. A shadow emerged behind him while Babatunde investigated the clue. The shadow started to move. And said, "I'm coming for you..."

Haris Sayanthan (13)
Greenford High School, Southall

THE PHONE CALL

"Hello! Hi I'm Ally and I think someone's breaking into my house," Ally whispered.

"Ally, this is Sarah, I'm going to help you, okay? Lock your door and hide under your bed," Sarah said.

Ally did as she was told. She lay there in the complete darkness. She couldn't hear anything. Had it worked? She was too scared to see the call end. She prayed Sarah didn't call otherwise her ringtone would give her away. All there was to be heard was silence until... *Bzzz!* went Ally's phone. Sarah! Ally instantly froze. Her heart stopped beating. *Creeakkk!* Ally's door opened.

Bradley Mushambi (14)
Stoneygate School, Great Glen

GUILTY?

"Guilty!" the verdict rang out, words not quite sinking in. How could they think it was me? Though that evening was a smudge in my memory, I was sure I'd followed my ordinary routine. But the CCTV showed no one had entered the vault but me... A hand shepherded me toward the tomb-like cell. This couldn't be happening! "I didn't take anything, I swear!" The guard just snorted at my outburst in response, door slamming shut. The walls threatened to suffocate me. I couldn't have done it. I wasn't a thief! The doubts confused me. I couldn't have done it, right?

Lauren Wong (14)
Stoneygate School, Great Glen

GONE

There was a shadow at the door... The sneaky, mischievous robber came closer and closer and closer. *Click! Click!* He was trying to get in! With fear shivering aggressively down my almost paralysed body, I clambered rapidly up off the freezing, creaky, wooden floor. I scampered away in fright. Silence... Nothing... Was he gone? Did he hear me? *Click!* Oh no! I glanced through a window. I tried to make out the tall figure. He saw me... He started coming closer! My heart was going as fast as a race car. I looked nervously back. There he was...

Oliver Cadby-Lynch (12)
Stoneygate School, Great Glen

THE DAY MY LIFE CAME TO A STOP

"Guilty!" the aged lady exclaimed.

I suddenly saw black and my eyes began to close but I didn't go to sleep. Many thoughts rushed into my head and many of those thoughts were guilt. Butterflies entered my fearful belly and I didn't know where the butterflies came from. I was speechless. Devastated. Worried. A bunch of words entered my head. Was I dreaming? No, I wasn't. A man elevated above me. He looked like a guard but he was far from it. He had cuffs in his palm. I was placed in handcuffs but yet so far from jail.

Skylar Gill (14)
Stoneygate School, Great Glen

GONE

Neenaw neenaw... The sirens rang out all over the town. The armed response vehicles whizzed through the quiet streets and up to the alleyway, but no one was there. But there, what was that? There was the outline of something on the ground. But it wasn't a something, it was a somebody. Police rushed up to the man and called an ambulance. The knife wounds were easily seen. The police split up to cover the nearby area and outskirts of the settlement. The ambulance rushed up to the scene and when they turned around, he was gone.

Harry Surtees (14)
Stoneygate School, Great Glen

TWO-FACED GUN

I burst through the front door as my partner went round the back. The suspect stood there frozen. He charged at me before I could draw my gun. we got into a bloody fistfight. To my relief, my partner walked in with his gun drawn but not on the suspect... On me. I gave him a look of pure pain and sadness. My friend of many years would be the one I would die by. He only said a few words to me as I stared down the barrel of his gun. "I'm sorry but this just has to happen..." *Bang!*

Josh Martin Sweeney (13)
Stoneygate School, Great Glen

THE CORRIDOR

It was cold. I was finally let out of my detention. Most of the lights had been turned off. Most of the staff had left and gone home. I was the only one in for a late detention. It was finally the end of it. I was on my way down a corridor with the light blinking on and off. A shadow was at the door, waiting for me. It had something sharp. The light flickered again. The shadow got closer to the door. Before I knew it, it was lights out...

Aryan Aziz (13)
Stoneygate School, Great Glen

NO ALIBI

Someone was dead. Someone was actually dead. And I know people don't just randomly drop dead. Suspicious behaviour had been going on like a virus around London. No, she wasn't just dead, she had been murdered. I thought that at any moment someone would open the door and shout, "Guilty!" There was a murderer on the loose, and I had no alibis to prove that I couldn't have done it.

Mia van Leeuwen (11)
Stoneygate School, Great Glen

THE TRAIN CHILD

"Jimy, nooo!" said Billy.

"No Billy," shouted Marie.

Poof! "Wow Jimmy, how did you do that? I just saw you get... get run over," said Billy in shock.

"I am just waiting for my mum," Jimmy said quietly. "She always says to stay where I am when I get lost so that's what's I'm doing?" Jimmy said, looking confused.

Marie looked over and saw a photo and flowers. "Jimmy, I'm sorry to tell you this but you're a ghost, look over there."

A tear rolled down his cheek. "How though?" Jimmy cried out.

"You got run over by a train."

Ludmila Kobiera (12)
The Willink School, Burghfield Common

THE ACCIDENT

Manslaughter, first-degree murder and second-degree murder are all terrible things. First thing that comes to mind is death and killing. What about if you add the word 'accidental' in front of it. 'Accidental killing' doesn't sound right. Well, it's going to because it happened yesterday.
A girl called Candice did this. A man by the name of Rick died because of this girl. Rick dropped his gun while running. The girl aimed to threaten the man and accidentally killed him. This girl was dead the next day with a sticky note on her back saying: 'We all make mistakes'.

Taylor Robinson (13)
The Willink School, Burghfield Common

ONCE DEAD, ALWAYS DEAD

People think I'm dead. On Friday 23rd September my girlfriend went missing and that same night her mother was murdered in the kitchen. I even had an alibi. It wasn't enough though. So one night I went on a walk. I can't remember much except someone drugged me and I passed out. The next day I bought a newspaper with headlines saying: 'Sal Singh committed suicide'.
I need to find her. I found her in a log cabin but when I talked to her she said, "I can't go back."
"Why?" I asked.
She replied whispering, "I killed my mother."

Sophie Jubb (13)
The Willink School, Burghfield Common

THE MISSING CHILDREN

"Come on Dan, Mum said we need to be back half an hour ago!" but something caught the twins' eyes, a dozen tall, frozen, inhuman figures, some climbing trees, others holding what looked like a tennis ball as if they were playing catch. "Who are they? And... why are they frozen?"

It was a sea of faceless mannequins. James, the bravest of the two, went to have a closer look. A piercing scream filled the air. They were the missing children, positioned to look like they were playing. They were murdered! The killer had struck again.

Charlie Chapman (12)
The Willink School, Burghfield Common

THE RIOT

Fierce flames fly in the sky. Sirens wail. My vision blurs. Rocks, bricks and bottles are thrown. I can't escape. We can't hold them back. They won't stop. Guns open fire. People drop. I stand, blood dripping from my face. I run. I can't stop. Then I feel it. It seeps through my shirt, spreading like a disease. I can't breathe. I collapse. I lose all feeling. I hear people, I hear them shout but I don't listen. I can't. I'm pulled. Pulled onto a stretcher. Cars screech to halt. People's shouts cut short. This is the end.

Nathan Audsley (13)
The Willink School, Burghfield Common

UNSOLVED

Suddenly, the air raid horn goes. We need to move now!
We run outside wondering if he's going to make it... I am
relaxing when I get a call saying, "Come quick!"
When I get there I realise something's wrong. My colleague
says that he was told there was a murder. There's nobody,
just a note.
A note saying: 'Give me a million otherwise I kill him'. There's
a passport taped to the bottom of the paper for a person
named Harry. I realise we need to work quickly otherwise we
will lose our best agent.

Ewan Morgan (12)
The Willink School, Burghfield Common

THE TWISTED DEATH

"Her death still haunts me to this day. Every morning when I wake up, every night before I sleep. It was around 4pm, me and Harriet were walking home from school when that figure appeared. Dressed all in black with a knife in their hand. They took her down an alleyway I went looking for her and then I saw her, covered in blood, not breathing. I couldn't believe my eyes. My best friend had been murdered..." That's my witness report to the police. They'll never know the truth and that is that I killed my sister, Harriet.

Molly Yeardley (13)
The Willink School, Burghfield Common

TAKEN

16th June 2028. I'm at home watching innocent people's lives being taken. The city is collapsing. I'm wondering when I will get taken, sent back to where I came from. *Drip, drip...* The ceiling whistles as I watch in fear. *Bang! Bang!* It's time. I see a kaleidoscope of colours as the door bursts open. My head is spinning in circles. Darkness. I rise from my slumber in a dark, empty room, cold and lifeless. I feel frozen. I see a masked officer with a weapon. I am lifeless. I cannot do anything. This is it. It's over.

Samuel Lambourne (13)
The Willink School, Burghfield Common

MY ESCAPE TO PRISON

The sand was blistering my feet as I sprinted across, surely it couldn't be. Yep, Morocco County prison officers coming right at me. How had they found me? I ran to my resource shed, grabbed my weights, attaching them to the duct tape tied on my dingy. I test ran the engine and pulled it out to the other side of the island. I gathered all my mangos and bananas and set sail. I'd gone 16 miles before I used my weight anchor and rested.
Sunrise came. I woke. This doesn't look like my dingy? I turned... Morocco County Prison.

Beth Cook (13)
The Willink School, Burghfield Common

ANOTHER DAY...

Another day, another case, I thought to myself. This one was different, they found her body. 27-year-old, Clair Hay, had been found dead. She had worked for me for three years before her disappearance. I never really liked her, she was just bossy, I don't think she liked me that much. As I strolled through the evidence I felt a crush of grief go through me. There wasn't that much to look at really. It just seemed like a drunken mistake, like she had hit her head. That's when I knew I would never be caught.

Holly Brown (13)
The Willink School, Burghfield Common

THE DEAD MAN

The body was in the middle of the road, with a torn piece of fabric stained with blood. I radioed for backup. "I need assistance on Bakers Street, forensic team and armed response please." I examined the body, their throat was slit and they had multiple torso wounds. When morning came, the street was shut off. The forensic expert, Josh Ward arrived on scene to examine deeply for any traces of anyone other than him. He said, "There are multiple fingerprints of our suspect Leo Baker."
"Need backup and all units, now!"

Devon Baggs (13)
The Willink School, Burghfield Common

THE HEIST

I couldn't stop running. I felt gunshots ricochet off the walls. I reached a wall and crouched behind it. The heist wasn't over, they were scenting me out, then I heard footsteps. I used my training to trip one over, knocking him out. One down, four to go. I had brought a lot of attention to myself and just made it to a pillar across the bank. I managed two well-aimed shots, two left. A gunfight broke out. I did the best I could but they hit my leg. I collapsed, they took all the gold they could carry and escaped.

Freddy Durrant (12)
The Willink School, Burghfield Common

THE DEEP WOODS

I was running to my house as I heard a screaming noise coming from the woods. I stopped and I was shocked, I didn't know what to do. I walked into the creepy, dark woods and saw someone lying on the floor. He was screaming for help, he was tied to the tree and was badly injured. Suddenly we both heard someone coming through the crunchy leaves. Suddenly the man approached and shouted, "Hey, if you make another sound I will hit you again."
I stuttered and tried to run away for help, but the man saw me...

Ollie Sebright (13)
The Willink School, Burghfield Common

THE MESSAGES

I got home, I called for my daughter but there wasn't a response. I got a message saying: 'If you don't obey my every word I will kill your daughter and tell everyone what you did'.

I was scared, but I knew I had to obey. He told me to go to my door. I found a cake, it said: 'Take me to this address... 74 Wall Street'. I got in my car and went to the address, dropped it off and left.

I got a message saying: 'Your daughter is dead and look what your cake did to her'.

Arthur Harvey (12)
The Willink School, Burghfield Common

THE FREAKY FISH

Neon red and blue lights flashed on the police cars that pulled in the car park. "There they are!" they heard from outside.

Zara and Zoe had always wanted a pet fish, but they were too poor to afford to buy one. Late one night Zara phoned Zoe to ask her to rob the aquarium with her as she'd watched Finding Nemo and decided she needed a fish, and she needed one now.

So that is what they did, they stole 14 goldfishes and then they ran to the van they pulled up in. Luckily they got there in time.

Jasmine Turner (13)
The Willink School, Burghfield Common

THE HITMAN

Bang! I am a criminal. My whole life's work has led to this point. My first paid hit and it won't be my last. The adrenalin of the shot and the escape, the sprint back to the car, the hope of not being seen. As I jump into the now dead man's Ferrari this will become the first of my collection. I've always had a thing about supercars and Ferraris are my favourite. Wounded. This is my final job. My last breaths as I bleed out, left to die. It's over. My legacy. My life.

Kai McKenna (13)

The Willink School, Burghfield Common

THE HEIST CRIME

Two men dead, lying on the floor and I had no knowledge about the crime. As much as I was confused, I started to hear the bank bell and suddenly I knew what it was... A heist. I ran over to the bank and asked questions and checked the cameras and found out a lot of information. I went back to the dead bodies knowing that there were four people robbing the bank but two were sacrificed or purposely killed, the other two and escaped through the sewer. I went down the sewer but the rats had killed them.

Luis John Alexander (13)
The Willink School, Burghfield Common

THE SHOOTING

Bang, bang, bang! I heard all the doors click shut. What was going on? I was in the library when I heard the bangs (which I now know as gunshots). It turns out they were coming from right outside the library door. I didn't know it was a shooting until I saw a shadow of a man holding a gun. I stopped what I was doing and darted to the safest place in the library. I thought of the librarian's office. I scrambled under the desk, pushing my back against the wall and squeezing my eyes shut...

Ava Standen (13)
The Willink School, Burghfield Common

MY TEARS TURN INTO BLOOD

My suffering caused him joy, my death would have brought him an advantage. So I killed him. They went down one by one, escaped to their deaths one after the other, all because of him. He didn't approve of the power women began to hold. He couldn't face the idea that the opposite gender, the so-called weak ones had the chance to be braver and stronger than him. The moment any female became a threat, their necks met the knife, a harsh death, isn't it? Well, that's how I killed him.

Michele Bros (13)
The Willink School, Burghfield Common

DETECTIVE RAHAL

Where is he? This is our mission, we can't fail. Let's hunt this criminal down. Our clues are, he went missing yesterday and he lives in a white house. The town is relatively small, we can get him. Let's go. I have eyes on a possible suspect dressed in black and looking suspicious. We have our man. "Run! Run!" I said. He's in a car now, this is a chase. After a very long car chase I am very proud to say Detective Rahal has solved the case! And I have won a leader award!

Rahul Thomas (13)
The Willink School, Burghfield Common

ACCIDENT

It was an accident... Those words found me guilty of one of the world's most horrible murders. It all started last week when I was working at a construction site. Normally I work from 5am to 5pm but today it was to 8pm. Once I finished work I drove home, but on the way home a black figure came out of nowhere and I had no time to stop. I was hoping it was just a deer but once I stepped out I could tell it wasn't. Tears gushed out of my eyes and suddenly something clicked. Dig!

Alexander Lee (13)
The Willink School, Burghfield Common

SET-UP

In the middle of the night a man let his dog out to go to the toilet. His dog ran into the woods. He went looking for him. He found him digging. He helped him dig. There was a body. It was still warm. He looked around to see if anyone was there then he checked out the body. It was his business partner. He saw a shiny thing. He picked it up. As he picked it up there was a bright light. Someone had taken a picture of him. Then he realised it was a set-up. "Nooo!"

Jon-Lee Cole (13)
The Willink School, Burghfield Common

THE DREAM OF A FUGITIVE

I have an alibi, but I'm scared I'm going to get caught so I'll have to run. I grab my keys and a few other bits and leave. I start the car and drive on an endless road. I turn on the radio and turn on the news. I have been found out! I pick up the speed and check my mirrors. I'm fine for now. I come across a motel. I'd better stay here for now. I pay for my room and head up to it. I turn on my TV and... I wake up. What happened?

Grace Uren (13)
The Willink School, Burghfield Common

BLOODY MARY

"Argh! Mary Stop it, please!"

Mary heard her best friend's screams again, as she stared into the creepy motel bathroom. Suddenly she saw blood-printed hand marks burying the mirror. The filthy, stained shower curtain rustled. Mary had just been divorced because of her endless cheating, just like she had cheated her best friend's life... Then she heard tapping on the window.

In disbelief, she washed her face, still not believing in the hallucinations. As she glanced back up to the mirror it was not her reflection, it was Elizabeth's... "Long time no see; I think it's your turn now..."

Eva Burden (12)
Wyvern St Edmund's, Laverstock

SUSPECT NUMBER THREE

"So, who do you think did it, Sam?"

Detective Sam replied, "Well, it's hard to tell but from the fingerprints left on the victim's glasses I think it could possibly be suspect number three."

"Really? Are you sure, Sam?"

"Quite sure," Sam lied. "I also have evidence from the footprints left in the pool of dried blood that came from the body. Yes, I am quite sure, John."

"Well, okay then, if you say so." John circled neatly around the name and picture of the innocent suspect number three. Sam smiled happily to herself, nobody would ever know.

Alice Johnson (12)
Wyvern St Edmund's, Laverstock

HIDE-AND-SEEK

A little girl excitedly calls out, "Come out, come out wherever you are!" She runs around the back garden looking behind trees, bushes and even under the table. Her mother opens the door telling her, "Dinner's ready, who are you playing with?" she asks, assuming it's their pet dog. "As always, found you," she says pointing into thin air, giggling.
"Sweetie, there's no one there." As she turns her head slightly to face her daughter, nothing but thin air. She can hear giggling in the distance and squints to see the swing set swinging back and forth, back and forth...

Lucy Reynolds (14)
Wyvern St Edmund's, Laverstock

DIDN'T MEAN TO DO IT...

She hadn't meant to do it. She just couldn't control them anymore. Anyway, no one would ever know what happened that night. She turned around, looking at the fire blazing high. That was when she realised the voices were gone. They had finally left. She smiled, then laughed maniacally. Her silhouette as dark as coal.

Six months later she was driving away from her latest victim's house, where plumes of smoke were rising continuously. Then, out of nowhere, red and blue lights came up behind her. She panicked, accidentally jolting the steering wheel. The car skidded, a cliff coming closer...

Charlotte Sims (12)

Wyvern St Edmund's, Laverstock

HALLUCINATION

"Dinner's nearly ready!" exclaimed the mum. The little sister ran down the stairs ready to eat. The man was already sitting down watching TV. "Stew again for dinner," said the mum as she handed three plates out.

"Thank you, Mummy," the little sister said gratefully.

"Eat up, eat up!" the mum said as she proceeded to stuff her face.

The man sighed with relief at how happy and lucky he was to have such a perfect family. His neighbours knocked on the door and decided to tell him the truth. "Your wife and daughter passed a long time ago."

Summer Pearce (14)

Wyvern St Edmund's, Laverstock

THE UNWANTED GUEST

I heard footsteps coming closer even though I was home alone. My mum answered the phone. "Someone is in the house!" I panicked.

"Do you trust me?" she asked.

"Yes..." I spoke, my voice trembling.

"Go to the guest bathroom, lock yourself in. Only family know it's there," she muttered.

I did as she said. "I'm in and I have the key in my hand. I'm in the bath," I whispered.

"Oh Rhea, can you really trust me?" she questioned.

"Yes," I spoke confidently.

"You shouldn't always trust everyone," she laughed as the door swung open aggressively and I screamed...

Charlotte Downer (13)
Wyvern St Edmund's, Laverstock

THE FOREST

"Are you sure we should be here?" Rachel asked nervously. Numerous people had disappeared in this forest over the last few weeks.

"Of course," Joey replied without a speck of fear in his voice. The sky got darker and the stars seemed to vanish as they travelled deeper into the forest.

Further ahead there was an orange glow between two trees. "Look, there's a fire!" Rachel exclaimed, running towards it to warm up. *Snap!* A branch snapped behind Rachel causing her to jump. "Joey?" He had vanished. Suddenly he jumped out from behind the trees, pushing her into the flames.

Emilie Reece (13)
Wyvern St Edmund's, Laverstock

KIDNAPPING

I lived by the park, one day walking through I heard a scream. I had found a crime scene, two children, the age of four and six had been kidnapped. I heard police say, "The suspect's gone." I heard the mother crying about her children.

Police finally found a witness and looked at CCTV. Someone shouted out, "I've found a clue." We finally found more clues to help but no sign of anyone who looked suspicious.

"My children!" the mother shouted out.

"At least we found the children."

When we find this man he is going to jail.

Anabelle Bosworth (14)

Wyvern St Edmund's, Laverstock

THE GRAVEDIGGERS

"He has to be somewhere!" Ben yelled.
After hours of researching the gravedigger's latest victim, there was no trace of him.
"Where in the world is Bones!" Ben yelled again.
"Pottery class," Lisa said calmly.
"Why do you call Lydia 'Bones' in the first place?"
"She studies bones and whatnot, when will she be back?" Ben said frustrated.
"Guys! Guys!" Carlos said running in out of breath. "He has her and he wants 10 million pounds for her location," he got out in one breath.
"What do you mean?" they questioned.
"She has 24 hours to live..."

Lizzie Bolton (12)
Wyvern St Edmund's, Laverstock

THE THING

Jack didn't know. No one told him, no one warned him, and his end was surely near. Jack walked into the woods, unaware of what might hit him. A hard grip surrounded the handle of his torch. Jack Whyler walked into the woods, the autumn leaves cracking under his feet. He was unaware of the danger he was in crossing through the woods. *Brr! Brr!* went his phone as he took it out of his pocket. "Unknown caller... Umm..." he said to himself. He considered hanging up but ended up responding by picking up. "Hello?" he asked.

"Turn around..."

Isaac Wright (11)
Wyvern St Edmund's, Laverstock

LOST AND FOUND

The oblivious officer turned away for a second, in a blink of an eye the suspect disappeared. The man was being tricked, he was intrigued to go on this riot. As the trees angrily swayed, lightning had struck a bush next to him. He scaredly said as he freaked out, "W-what a coincidence." The pitch-black nights had frightened the life out of him. As it was getting gloomier a shadow approached the man and creepily spoke, "Goodnight." *Bang!*
The suspect was never seen again. The next year, a man was found digging the police officer out of his grave...

Sofia Manicom (12)
Wyvern St Edmund's, Laverstock

RITUAL OR MURDER?

Lying in bed, I thought about the murderer on the loose, already forty-nine lives taken in two weeks. The next morning, I tried to help find a missing child. I heard a muffled voice shout over the radio, "We caught him, the murderer!" When I arrived, I was shocked, seeing strange markings on the walls. The murder kept muttering, "Fifty!" He was insane... Fifty lives? Fifty bodies? Whatever it was, it was over now.

Lying in bed once more, I thought about the markings, almost like a ritual, I reassured myself by repeating, "It's not like spirits are real... right?"

Carla Carpenter-Paya (11)
Wyvern St Edmund's, Laverstock

TECHNOLOGICAL CONTROL

Who am I? What's my purpose? But why does it matter when technology is in control of me. Everywhere at all times. I remember when the world was different, I felt free. I could do what I wanted and express who I really was. Cameras everywhere, placed wherever possible. No one to tell me what's right and wrong. The government is in control of everyone. Vulnerable people are manipulated to do whatever they say. Anger builds up, I clench my fists at the thought of technology intimidating people. But I'm the technological control in this story. I am the camera.

Helena Peska (14)
Wyvern St Edmund's, Laverstock

WHO'S NEXT?

Shatter! A window had smashed; it came from downstairs. Stalking out my room I noticed glass on the stairs. Stepping around, I looked at the room I was in, noticing a blood-red envelope on the counter in the kitchen. Walking over, gingerly I opened the envelope. 'An ocean blue-eyed girl' was all it said. *Bang!* The door slammed. An ocean blue-eyed girl? What did that mean? I looked around me once again. Something was missing, but what? Nothing looked out of place. Until my eyes reached the mantelpiece... It was missing. The necklace I had left out...

Tarian Nix (12)

Wyvern St Edmund's, Laverstock

A SINGLE SUSPECT

"We learned, that at 12:32 Sunday, Mrs Lacock was brutally murdered. Our initial, and only suspect, Mr Lacock. He had motive, he had the chance, it was sure to be him... But he also had an alibi. With no other suspects, our only option was to research the crime scene. As you all know from previous discussions, the killer left no evidence and no fingerprints. However, after further inspection, we discovered one small discrepancy. A button. Mrs Almsdale, would you, Mrs Lacock's housekeeper, care to explain to us how one of your shirt buttons ended up under her sofa?"

Alice Ewen Benns (14)
Wyvern St Edmund's, Laverstock

THE MASS MURDER

The police turned up to a murder scene but what they didn't know was that this case would be bigger than they expected... They found the original murdered body. Whilst looking for evidence one of the officers discovered something unusual. What the officer saw was another body, then another, and another. Soon he realised this had become a bigger case. He radioed to his fellow officers and explained all that had been seen. Later on, more police arrived. They followed the trail of bodies and found a cave. They went in and found a man. They had found their murderer.

George Nash (13)
Wyvern St Edmund's, Laverstock

COUNTDOWN

The arsons started seven days ago. "We have reason to believe your house will be targeted next. We already have six suspects."
"Really?"
"Each house that has been set alight has number five on that road. We need to get you away from here."
Four people had died; three arsons had happened. Me and my partner were at the place we thought would be targeted next, speaking to the person who lived there. Just us two detectives. The person stood and suddenly ran out the house. We smelt burning, saw fire and... Oh, the one last 'victim' was the arsonist.

Alice Natelson-Carter (13)
Wyvern St Edmund's, Laverstock

DON'T LISTEN

Silence. Complete utter silence. All I could hear was my heart thumping, hands shaking, mind racing. The sky was dark but still no stars, the grass so cold it almost felt wet. For one second on this soul-changing night, I felt a pause. Then the stillness was shaken. Flashing lights arose over the horizon and all the voices rushed in again. I scrambled to my feet and ran, all I could do was run. As I ran I kept telling myself, *don't listen, resist your response*, under my breath. *Don't listen, resist your response.* I couldn't. I'd been caught.

Sienna Searle (14)
Wyvern St Edmund's, Laverstock

THE MISSING PERSON

The police headquarters went inaudible, something must have gone awfully wrong for the police headquarters to go this noiseless. On the screen of Sargeant John's there popped up a massive sign reading: 'A prisoner has escaped from death row', the name read Elijah Williams. First thought that went through their heads was the attempted assassination of the Queen and her beloved husband. The alarm was sounded. The village was on lockdown.
A few weeks went by. The police lined the streets. No one was seen for weeks. Not even Elijah Williams...

Ella-Louise McCartney (12)
Wyvern St Edmund's, Laverstock

THE SHADOW

She knew who it was, she knew but she couldn't say. No, no, she could never say. She turned to the shadow, there so she followed the rules. A shadow, for that is all you could call it. With its hunched yet towering frame, its dripping jaws now stretched into a ferociously grim smile. She turned again to face the officer. "No, I didn't see anything last night." Her eyes attempting to portray the desperate cry for help. But he turned away. With one last forlorn look over her shoulder towards her grisly beast of a companion, she turned too.

Hannah Waterworth (14)
Wyvern St Edmund's, Laverstock

GUILT

I know what I did. Guilt is all I felt. Something inside me craved it. The monster being me. I try to neglect it, but it's levitating. Looming. Lurking. You don't relate? Must not be as crazy as I am. I remember the day. The body. The blood. The memory, seemingly seducing me. With its silky rouge pulling me into its tenacious void. It was here again, not gently tugging at my sleeve, but dragging me. Its dictatorial grasp on my ankles. That scream. The scarlet blood. My knife sinking into her marshmallow skin. The bruising a violent, vicious violet...

Sophie Ollivierre (14)
Wyvern St Edmund's, Laverstock

THE DEAD

Karly knew she was... different. The first time Karly saw things was age five, outside the house he stood, black clothing painted in his own thick red blood. The next time was fourteen, again he stood, this time outside her English classroom. A woman now stood with him both covered in scars, their faces hid from view. After that she saw them regularly, she knew no one else could see them. Each time the scarred figures crept closer. When Karly turned nineteen they appeared in her room. Finally, she could see their faces. There stood her dead parents.

Laura Massie (14)
Wyvern St Edmund's, Laverstock

ASYLUM

I reached my arm across the neatly laid table to pass my grandad the fresh salad.

"Cheers David."

"No problem, Grandad."

"I will have some of that too," Mum interfered.

Grandad passed her the bowl and she smiled at him to show gratitude. Chase, the small, white dog barked as if to say 'give me some'.

"Shush, Chase." Grandad gave him a potato and he ran away with it into his bed. We all laughed. These family dinners were my favourite...

I was woken from my dream by a knock at my door. The nurse gave me my evening meal.

Molly Williams (14)
Wyvern St Edmund's, Laverstock

UNARMED MURDER

It was 11 at night when private detective, Stephen Chard stumbled across the murder scene. The clouds were angrily spitting at the Earth. Thunder clouds rolled over the steep hills. The black Mercedes rolled into the car park and Stephen got out. As Stephen walked over, he saw the body. The victim was bleeding from a straight slash across their body. He saw something move suddenly inside the alleyway and went to check it out. Five minutes later he came out, pale with grey eyes. "I-it was a-a..." Then he splurted some blood from his mouth. He died.

Oliver Leak (13)
Wyvern St Edmund's, Laverstock

CANNIBAL

Cold water shot out of the tap in the holding cell, he put his hand under the water, washing away the sticky red substance from his fingers. Cupping his now clean hands, gathering water before splashing it around his mouth, blood and chunks of flesh falling down into the sink. Behind him was the mangled form of a woman.

The next day, he entered the police precinct again. He was met with the sight of his panicking co-workers. "What's wrong?" he asked.

"The suspect is dead! Any idea as to who did it?"

He bit back a smile. "No." Lie.

Fern Shearer (12)
Wyvern St Edmund's, Laverstock

THE MYSTERIOUS MURDER

"This is BBC News, last night at 13 Downing Street, there was a murder. Franklin Smith died. The prime suspect is Warren Smith."

"Just going out for work Jess, I'll be back at 10 o'clock, be a good girl."

Still, at 10:30 she hadn't come back, she heard a car pull up at her drive. It was a new car she hadn't seen before. A figure wandered out of the car. He opened the door, her mum didn't lock it. The creak of the stairs made her hide under the covers. The door flung open. He pulled up his mask...

Stanley Maculewicz (11)
Wyvern St Edmund's, Laverstock

THE FUNERAL

I walked into the church and sat on a bench. John walked to the front where a picture of Jenna Tonkin sat. "Thank you for coming to say goodbye to Jenna," he said smiling sadly at the wider room. It was a small ceremony I thought as John talked about her achievements. As the time went on I noticed my vision becoming hazy. I blinked rapidly turning around, seeing everyone else doing the same. I stood up, my movements sluggish. The doors banged open as my legs collapsed. A person bent down gripping my chin... "Together forever," Jenna whispered.

Jessica Teltow (13)
Wyvern St Edmund's, Laverstock

MY FAVOURITE COLOUR

Her red velvet blood danced like ribbons. Thimblefuls a second, enough for my pleading eyes. In agony she cried, entreating to stay. Unfortunately today was our special last day. Should I leave her be or was this 'villain' really me? These sinking violet bruises I fed; creating a beautiful contrast with the velvet blood she bled. I hummed to her screams, sang to her sobs. Then I realised, then I knew, the pain I'd inflicted hurt me more than her. The red blood she bled in the dark would shine. Red wasn't her favourite colour, but it was mine.

Grace Harwood (13)
Wyvern St Edmund's, Laverstock

A NEW FRIEND

"Bye, see you tomorrow!"
As she walked back home, she noticed a picture on the floor in front of her. It was a familiar face. Slowly she picked it up and one word stood out... 'Wanted'. She was speechless. She ran home in fear. The paper was scrunched up in her hand. "Mum! Mum!" Grace shouted, panicking.
"What is it, honey?"
Grace explained how she had been with the man in the paper for weeks. Her mum looked at the picture and broke into tears. "Why! That man killed your father!"

Anita Biju (12)
Wyvern St Edmund's, Laverstock

KIDNAPPED

"What's my name?" I queried, dizzily. I attempted to walk down a moonlit hall until I stumbled into someone's arms. They questioned, "Are you okay?"
I tried to answer but all I could say was, "N-n-no!"
As he was about to respond there was a knock on the door. The man grabbed me with his hands as cold as ice, he pulled me to the door. Creaking it opened. It was the police, they pondered, "Have you seen this girl, she's missing?" while showing an image.
I thought for a while until I got a sense, familiarity. It was me!

Ben Millman (14)
Wyvern St Edmund's, Laverstock

THE ANONYMOUS ANIMAL ATTACK

I just didn't understand, how was Tyler Robinson a vampire, a monster that drinks human blood? He looked and acted normal but sometimes he acted weird around Isaac Routledge, his friend.

A couple of weeks passed. I decided not to worry about it until one day I came across Isaac eating a human. I thought to myself, *has Tyler turned him into a vampire?* I raced home, turned on the news. It said several bodies had been found supposedly bitten by an anonymous animal but I knew who did it. Until this day they don't know I know.

Shelby Roxburgh (13)
Wyvern St Edmund's, Laverstock

BLOOD BARN

The suspect was gone, orchestrated a riot and was out like a cat in the night, confessing that he committed the murder just to lead us on, only thing left was a paper saying: 'Guilty' signed 'A'. We knew this was enough to convict him. Patrol cars out every night, a number to call if we saw suspicious activity. Soon enough we got him. "Mysterious person in black, with a girl, walking into a barn."
Ten minutes later a gunshot and scream. They rushed to the barn. The woman who called saw written in her blood: 'I'm still here. A'.

Amy Marshall (12)
Wyvern St Edmund's, Laverstock

THE DIM FOREST

Come on, let's go in the dim forest," she said.
"No, something bad could happen," I said.
Next thing we knew we were lost in a dim wood. "What did I tell you!" I shouted.
She said, "I'm so sorry, what was that? Argh!"
"What?"
She was there, dead. Suspected murder. The suspect was a man named Tom Cowhat. His fingerprints matched those on the weapon.
He is now in prison for life, read the newspapers and the news on TV. I know not to go in there. My friend is dead. Why? Why my best friend? It's not fair.

Ella Becker (11)
Wyvern St Edmund's, Laverstock

THE MISSING HEAD

A flash shot through the jet-black windows of Edington Airport, at the same time an eye-watering shriek came from a jet. Security came, picked up a man. But, with no head. Police tracked footprints to a gloomy warehouse. The sound of crunching bones echoed. They went inside. A body, but no head. A crack came from a corner. A police officer was pushed out. He walked to a corner but never came back. When they found the body, no head. Nobody came out of the warehouse that night.

If you do go, you may scream but nobody will come.

Fergus Sime (12)

Wyvern St Edmund's, Laverstock

A MURDER IN THE MAKING

A murderer was lurking about in the city of Salisbury, killing someone each night and hiding them from existence. Nobody knew where or who this person was except the killer and the souls of the murdered. A few days later police had suspicious thoughts about a woman who took blood-red liquid to work every day since the people went missing. She said that it was pure cranberry juice but no one believed her so the police went in to investigate. It was an early Monday morning when they went in but the lady wasn't there. Was she killed?

Joseph Holme (12)
Wyvern St Edmund's, Laverstock

THE RAILWAY

It was a misty day in London. Mark and James were at their favourite place to go, the railway. Mark and James would go there often, until they never went again. They were at the railway when Mark heard a scream from inside an abandoned train. He went to look what it was, leaving James behind. When he was in the area he thought he heard the scream. James shouted, "Help!" He left and started sprinting. When he got there James was gone and all the police found was a severed finger. Mark still hears James screaming for help.

Bradley Stewart (12)
Wyvern St Edmund's, Laverstock

FINGER FOR A FINGER

"Guilty!" Words echoed over the court. I tapped four fingers to the desk. A sobbing wife screamed with relief, poor Gwen. Man found missing hand, in New Forest. An old mate of mine, so the case came into my hands. What a relief now it's all over. He was a good fella, how I lost my finger actually. Good times. Home, comforting place. Flipping off my shoes, a grin danced across my face. I leant over, clasping my cold old friend. I strapped that beautiful new finger on. The door creaked open, my hand raised. "Do you like it, Gwen?"

Olivia Harris (14)
Wyvern St Edmund's, Laverstock

MY BEST FRIEND

As a police officer slowly stumbled into the classroom he announced that Trish, my best friend, had been killed and the murderer had not been found yet. Everyone's faces in the class went all gloomy and depressed as well as mine. But that was not the emotion I was feeling! I was happy, ecstatic on the inside that me, Emma, could get away with murder. You might be wondering why I killed her? What drove me to it? She was my best friend, wasn't she? Well, I killed her for one reason and one only... She stole my water bottle.

Gabriella Manicom (12)
Wyvern St Edmund's, Laverstock

HUSBAND STEW

You know you should keep safe at these times, especially with these murders going on. These were the words that were going on and on in my mind. I finally snapped myself out of my thoughts with the last words from the officer. "I'm sorry about your husband's murder Ma'am."
With the power I had left in me I shut the door and walked into the kitchen. I was cooking some stew. "He was a useless husband and anyway he was supposed to be cooked."
Silence was all that could be heard but then this... "You'll be next!"

Kara Lyons (12)
Wyvern St Edmund's, Laverstock

MISTAKES

The room was drenched in blood, Arthur's hands covered in the blood of another one of his parent's mistakes. Arthur peered over to the wall full of photos of the mistakes his parents had made... He had to remove the ones who made his life a misery, everything had to be perfect. If it wasn't it had to be removed. The apartment stank of rotting flesh. He looked over to the bathroom door, the blood ran slowly from under the door. She was only ten, the poor girl... No one knew such an 'innocent' boy could do such despicable things.

Hannah Reader (14)
Wyvern St Edmund's, Laverstock

THE UNEXPECTED WALK

It was a normal sunny day after school when two best friends, Jess and Jazz were walking home. They turned around the corner and started walking down the path and unexpectedly they bumped into some very dodgy people. They started to walk faster and then started to run. They ran for miles. They were safe, well they thought they were. They decided to start walking towards their houses so they could be safe. They were both out of breath, and just walked around the corner when they heard them... He pulled a gun out of his pocket...

Jessica Jackson (13)
Wyvern St Edmund's, Laverstock

THE VOICE

Elizabeth shouldn't have been left at home. She played with her toys but she heard something. "Come closer!" She went on playing, not paying attention. "I see you," it said again. This time Elizabeth's heart started to race. A key turned in the lock but it was only her mum back from the shops (or so she thought).

"Quick, get in the car!" her mum said so she leapt into the rusty car, not seeing the red stains on the seat. "I have you!" the voice said for the last time, but this time Elizabeth could see who was speaking.

Isabelle Malata (12)
Wyvern St Edmund's, Laverstock

THE MURDER OF MADDIE MOORE

He pulled the trigger. A bullet shot straight at her. She fell to the blood-covered floor. I awoke with a jolt. Taunted by my dream, I got out of bed and turned on the TV. "Breaking news! Maddie Moore has been found dead near Rosewood Valley with a gun wound to her chest."
I paused the TV. Maddie Moore, that sounded familiar. A flashback of my dream occurred. It didn't make sense. Why was this story so familiar? I felt a stab of panic. Surely I hadn't done it. I hadn't murdered Maddie Moore. Had I?

Amelia Weston (13)
Wyvern St Edmund's, Laverstock

THE PROMISED NEVERLAND

Another day in the orphanage. Me and Drista decide to go spy on Mother when she takes Connie through the gates to get adopted. We've never been allowed near the gates. Now we wait for the night to come. It's pitch-black and all of the orphans are saying goodbye to Connie. We sneak outside and follow the lantern. It's Connie and Mother! We follow them to the gates and they're both gone. But there's a parked van... We look inside the van and there Connie is, pale and lifeless. We find out the orphanage is a demon food farm...

Kaitlin Stewart (13)
Wyvern St Edmund's, Laverstock

EXPLOSIVE SURPRISE

It added up, he had to be here. I walked into the house. Everything looked like it'd survived a nuclear blast. I could hear beepers. It got louder the further I got into the house. I searched the house and I discovered a hidden loft (this was where the beeping was coming from). I climbed the ladder into the loft and I found a hostage lying up against a wall with duct tape over his mouth. I could hear him screaming with a muffled tone but suddenly I could hear the beeping getting faster and faster... "Wait..."

Ethan Reeve (13)
Wyvern St Edmund's, Laverstock

THE TRICK CASE

Something just didn't feel right, I looked down at the dead body. There were no stab wounds that the woman talked about and the blood looked too liquidy to be real. Something felt off. I just couldn't grasp what it was. I looked up at the crying woman. Her tears slowly rolled down each cheek. I was missing some key information but what that information was I didn't know. I turned to look at the clock and I heard two loud cackles. Before I could turn around a sharp pain went right through my heart. I was their next victim.

Eleanor Ollivierre (13)
Wyvern St Edmund's, Laverstock

CLASSROOM D3.7

"Let's go to English now," Ellie said to her friend.
"But we're still early, let's look in Class D3.7," replied Livvy.
So they opened the door and walked in. The window was open so they went to see outside of it. As they got to the window, it felt like they were being pulled vigorously by their heads. They started screaming, but no one could hear them. The next thing they knew they were in a small village in the middle of an isolated desert, in front of a big sign saying: 'Ellie and Livvy, wanted for murder'...

Coco Jones (14)
Wyvern St Edmund's, Laverstock

THE VOICES

My mum thinks I have imaginary friends. I think she means 'the voices'. I have to obey. They talk to me. My sister made me mad today, so the voices shrieked inside my head, *kill her!* They repeated over and over again. They told me to get a knife. She was gone. My impulses were too strong. I laughed at the scene, feeling accomplished. I'm too young for jail so I'm in hospital. People think it will help but I know the voices won't stop until everyone around is dead. I think Mum will be next. I'm not afraid though.

Niamh Ball (14)
Wyvern St Edmund's, Laverstock

REMORSE

One dark night two kids were pranking the people of London when they found a small house. They went inside to place down stink bombs and suddenly one of them tripped and a thud shook the building and then a woman with long hair and a mask walked in and sighed and grabbed the two kids and killed them. She gasped in guilt and walked to the basement crying, realising she'd murdered two innocent kids. She pulled out her phone and called the police and said two words, "I'm sorry," then she hanged herself on the washing line.

Evan Tonkinson (11)
Wyvern St Edmund's, Laverstock

PYROMANIA

Branches were burning, the body lay there cold and lifeless. Its decaying flesh and blood seeped into the soil below. Detective Sam Brooke had investigated the scene. He had a suspect. He walked back through the flaming woods. Back at the station he prepped for the interrogation of Jack Green, pyromaniac. "I know you did it, I saw you!" said Sam proudly.

Jack chuckled, "Okay ya got me, I killed 'em but it's your word against mine!" Jack whispered. "Ahaha, you thought you got me, better luck next time, Detective!"

Eva Hammond (11)

Wyvern St Edmund's, Laverstock

THE GHOST OF REVENGE

Maggie Turner found out that her husband, George Turner, cheated on her with his boss. This made her so enraged. She wanted revenge so decided to kill him. As she stabbed him his vermillion blood oozed out of him. She hid his corpse under her creaky floorboards.

As weeks slowly went past she began to regret her decision. One night, a really stormy night, Maggie felt a cold breeze flurry over her. This led to her being awoken. She sat up and at the end of her bed, he was there, holding a knife to her son's neck...

Hetty Gray (13)
Wyvern St Edmund's, Laverstock

THE DEAD KILLER

The body lay there worthless. Blood on my hands, on the walls, on my face, in my mouth. I enjoyed the taste, the sweetness, the sourness. I seemed to crave the blood. I couldn't control the hunger, it took over me. I lie next to the victim's neck and crunched through her skin, downing the blood. She was pale and empty, her body so light as she was skin and bone. I saw blue lights flashing around the corner, the sirens so deafening. My body moved, I was running, faster than usual. Then I remembered... I should be dead.

Olivia Glover (14)
Wyvern St Edmund's, Laverstock

THE KIDNAPPER

It was a nice calm night, not much was happening. Suddenly I looked up and saw an open window. I noticed a little boy. I scaled the building and grabbed the child. I sprinted to my blue Mercedes Benz and stuffed the child in the boot. I sped away into the night. Half an hour later, I had got to my hideout. I asked the child his name. He replied, "My name is Charlie."

"Hi," I replied.

I decided to turn on the TV. The news was on. The newsman calmly said, "The FBI has investigated and found the kidnapper..."

Reuben Leinster (12)

Wyvern St Edmund's, Laverstock

THE DOOR IN THE WOODS

There was a door standing alone in the woods once. No one ever dared to go near it, some even moved away after it had been discovered. But I was intrigued completely and utterly. It never made sense why it was there which was why I was so mesmerised by it. The chained-up door pulled me in. Someone disappeared once, I'm confident it was because of the door. I walked closer, my future decisions undecided. Suddenly the door was level with my eyes. I had been waiting much too long to see this. What was behind the door?

Bethany Alford (13)
Wyvern St Edmund's, Laverstock

IT WAS HIM!

The suspect was gone, Ben the detective was investigating the murder of Luke. Eventually, Simon the assistant arrived huffing and puffing his lungs out. Ben then took a swab of fingerprints and started to detect who it was. Then, in a blink of an eye, Simon injected venom through the flesh of Ben. Blood poured through his nose whilst his blood ran cold. Knocks from the door echoed through his ear. Simon rapidly escaped the house like a bounty hunter on the chase. Leaving the computer on with his face all over it...

Prerna Magenni (12)
Wyvern St Edmund's, Laverstock

THE CAMERA OF TRUTH AND DEATH

Once, a man saw a camera, he tried selling it but no one would buy it. He always tried to turn it on but it never worked but one day it worked. He could see everyone's darkest secrets but that wasn't the only thing he could see. He also saw a time. It looked liked 10 years. After nine years he was a wealthy and successful person, he still always kept the camera since it had been with him forever since he was homeless. When the time reached 0 he died. The camera also. Another ten years passed, the camera reappeared.

Jack Dewey (12)
Wyvern St Edmund's, Laverstock

THE ABC MURDER

One afternoon a group of girls walked to school. They heard noises but ignored them. It was a sunny day in Highfields. Eventually, they turned the corner but realised Ava was gone. They went back but there was nothing. But, out of nowhere the girls had bags over their heads and were thrown into a van. This man had taken them home and tied them to a chair in alphabetical order saying, "This is the order you die!" repeatedly with an evil laugh and smirk but then there was a knock at the door and a bang from a shotgun.

Jasmine Halliwell (13)
Wyvern St Edmund's, Laverstock

THE POISONED DRINK

The suspect was gone. Harold, a young man had poisoned his friend's drink. Jerald had no idea, he had poisoned it. Later, Jerald and Harold went to a bar. They both ordered the same drink. Jerald went somewhere that gave Harold a perfect chance to poison it. Jerald came back and decided he didn't want it. He gave it to someone else. Then he died dramatically. Jerald got accused of murder and soon went to jail. Harold made a run for it. Harold is still out there. Ready and prepared. The case is yet to be solved.

William Pearce (12)
Wyvern St Edmund's, Laverstock

DIFFERENT REALITY

You wake up with a strange feeling in your gut. You ignore it. Straight away, checking your phone, there is only one message: 'Trust nobody, it's not real. None of it is. Escape'. It's unsettling however you dismiss it as you walk into the living room then, standing in front of you is your whole family lined up, each with a slight frown on their face. Your 'mother' with the biggest frown of all. She tilts her head to the left. "You didn't receive anything strange this morning now did you? Nothing at all?"

Molly Taylor-Rice (11)
Wyvern St Edmund's, Laverstock

THE CRIME SCENE

The suspect was gone... I stared around at the bloodstained walls as the girl's body lay lifeless. Her eyes were gouged out and her head was cut off and placed next to her. I knew it was her father as if he was innocent he would never have left. I suddenly heard a loud noise from the room next door. I slammed open the door. He had killed himself. A note was written onto a receipt pinned to the table. The note read: 'I did not kill her, you will burn for this'. I knew then, her father was innocent.

Chloe Martin (13)
Wyvern St Edmund's, Laverstock

THE GIRL IN THE DISTANCE

It was a cold autumn night, and the street lights were flickering. I was walking home and all of a sudden, I saw a figure appear in the distance, running from a moving van. The figure was of a female, in her early teenage years (like me). She did a 180° turn to face the van. Her eyes turned yellow and she gradually lifted her head. Slowly, the van elevated. It dropped to the ground and she vanished into thin air. I rushed to the van and opened the crushed door. Five men with lab coats were inside, all dead.

Poppy Partridge (13)
Wyvern St Edmund's, Laverstock

THE DREAM

For years, Gerald had the same nightmare, he would wake up sweating. It felt so real. He thought about how it would haunt him again. In the nightmare it was dark and cold. He was standing in a hallway with people chained to the walls. He looked down into his hand and he had a blade. Gerald started killing people. He woke up, his heart pounding in a cold sweat. 6:45 he woke for work. He showered. He got breakfast. He brushed his teeth. He went to get his tie. He reached into his drawer, there was the blade...

Izabella Grand-Scrutton (12)
Wyvern St Edmund's, Laverstock

TWO YOUNG LOVERS...

"I love you forever, I promise." That's what he said. Just two young lovers in secondary. Elliot was falling for a girl in his set. I believe her name was Kaci. At break she told her friends and they asked him out for her. They got together the next day however Libby and Miley were annoying Kaci and teasing her. So Elliot had a smashing idea. "We should kill them!" Kaci agreed with the plan so at 11:30 on Monday they went for both of them. There was the sound of the knife on the floor and blood everywhere...

Miley Poulter (11)
Wyvern St Edmund's, Laverstock

THE CAMERA

The year was 1998. Sam was training to become a professional photographer. He was just 18, hoping for the job, so he got his camera and started. First, he took a picture of an apple then he took a bite. He printed out the picture only to find the picture had a bite in it. Confused, Sam took a picture of himself and printed it. His heart sank, in the picture, it was him in a dark alleyway with a knife in his chest and blood slowly dripping from his mouth. He started to panic as his front door creaked open...

Daniel Hawkes (12)
Wyvern St Edmund's, Laverstock

DEAR WORLD

Dear World, I confess I killed John Hopwood, I didn't mean to however I don't regret it. He walked through the door like nothing happened. Like what he'd done didn't bother him. I walked over to the kitchen and grabbed a knife and plunged it into his cold, loveless heart. I ran. I ran here to this bridge to confess. Not for what I did but how it feels. I think I need help because I feel so alive. Now I stand upon this bridge to say sorry for my doings and be with my love again. Dear world, goodbye forever.

Elizabeth Lord (14)
Wyvern St Edmund's, Laverstock

THE COLD BLADE

I heard the floorboard creak beneath my feet as I stepped blindly down the stairs. I needed to find them and teach them a valuable lesson. The last one that they would ever learn. I felt for the knife that was safely in its sheath. I was ready. I walked to the end of the corridor and turned the knob on the door. And then I heard it... A faint voice filled with triumph. "I've been waiting for this day!" it said.
I spun around but there was no one. Then I felt it. A cold blade in my back.

A Evans (13)
Wyvern St Edmund's, Laverstock

MURDER IN THE NIGHT

There were three siblings. Josh, Jake and Lily. They were playing in their room and Josh and Lily got into an argument. Their mum got angry and told them to go to bed. The next morning they woke up hoping that breakfast would be on the table. Josh was lying in bed with a cut through his neck. Later that day, when Lily was playing with her dog, who was called Suzie and had a little fluffy tail, Jake started tidying their room. When he was putting toys in her toy box he came across a knife with blood on...

Maddie Coombes (12)
Wyvern St Edmund's, Laverstock

ENDLESS LOOP

The sirens blared behind me as I ran through the thick woods. My legs ached as I forced myself to move faster, as it was either run or get mauled by police dogs. Trust me, I know. I've lived through this many times before, caught in an endless loop. The tall trees surrounded me, their arms, sharp as knives, cut at my skin as I raced away. I knew exactly where to go to end it, only to start again, the rivers. Where it always ends. Where my mind always resets itself. Here it always is. My own corpse.

Sydney Gape (14)
Wyvern St Edmund's, Laverstock

HE ESCAPED

All the parents locked their doors except one. She wasn't scared of the kidnapper but little did she know what was coming. She let her ten-year-old, Sarah, out to go play in the park and she never came back. Sarah went outside but no one was there so she just stood there confused and suddenly a man was there. He grabbed her tightly like he was not gonna let go. She was scared, she started shouting but before she knew it she was in a basement. The man came down with a gun. She was never seen again.

Eva Whittingham (11)
Wyvern St Edmund's, Laverstock

IMPOSTERS

A pound at the door. A ring of the bell. I stood up and walked to the door and saw two police officers. "Are you Miss Greenwood?"

"Yes, is something wrong?" I questioned, confused.

"We're sorry to tell you but we found the bodies of your family members in a ditch."

"Can't be!"

"We have fingerprints to prove it," said the other officer.

"Follow me," I trembled.

I took them to the dining room where the table was set. There sat my family, smiling. Hungry. Ready to eat.

Olivia Toms (14)

Wyvern St Edmund's, Laverstock

TRAPPED

The subject was gone and I was left in a dark room, glued to a chair with no escape route. I called out for help but no response came, only a horrifying squeal and then a gloomy figure appeared before me. It was wearing all black which made it invisible to the naked eye. It was also holding a sack. Before I could say a word another figure came from behind me and covered my mouth while I was struggling. The first figure pulled something out of its sack. Then the mysterious object began to beep...

Evelyn Lambert (13)
Wyvern St Edmund's, Laverstock

IT WAS TOTALLY A KIDNAPPING

My ma always remembers to lock every door and window in the house, this is because of what happened to my little sister. One night my mum 'forgot' to shut the windows of the house and in the morning my sister was gone. Ma says she was kidnapped and the person came in through the window. I don't think I will tell her that all the windows of the house were locked and I went into the basement with my sister and let's just say there is a little girl's body down there to this day.

Eloise (13)
Wyvern St Edmund's, Laverstock

THE PRISON

The morning started when three prisoners arrived at their cells. They saw a vent, they tried to climb into it but failed then they saw a new cop. They got hold of his prison keys, slowly they walked to the back door. They got out soon after. They came back for some reason then two hours later new cops came for their shift. Before opening the door they found a note that said: 'Don't enter or your lives will be changed forever'. They entered slowly. They found all the prisoners dead. They ran out.

Jack Whyler (12)
Wyvern St Edmund's, Laverstock

UNSOLVED

The suspect was gone behind the trees and was nowhere to be found. I began to worry that it may happen again, the same accident that happened last night, on a cold winter's night. The next thing I intended to do was to go and search for this man. I walked slowly and steadily trying not to make a sound. I looked behind trees until I saw footsteps leading to a house. It was dark so I couldn't see but I still went on. I got to the door, opened it and there he was, looking straight at me...

Chloe Guttridge (14)
Wyvern St Edmund's, Laverstock

ROOM 101

It all started in Room 101, in a hotel down the end of Crooky Street. Room 101 was kept by an old lady who had recently died. No one went into the room. Every night, if you stood across the road a ghost would stare out. One night a man decided to go into the room, only to come across a ghost lady following him as he walked around. As he left the ghost pulled him back and screeched, "You fell in my trap!" The door slammed and the man's disappearance became famous. Room 101 was soon blocked off.

Lily Burt (12)
Wyvern St Edmund's, Laverstock

THE DEAD MURDER

He looked at the house before he entered. The mist clouded over it. He went in and started to explore. He came across something, the body, lifeless on the floor. Near the body was a knife, he looked at it, it was dripping with scarlet-red blood. He picked up the knife and put it into a ziplock bag and sent it off to the lab for a DNA test. Sometime later, the results came back. It led back to one person. But it was impossible, they died twenty years ago. He could only come to one conclusion...

Abby Azzopardi (12)
Wyvern St Edmund's, Laverstock

THE GHOST BROTHER

People say the dead can't talk. Well, me and my family just moved into a house that was built on a graveyard. All of the lights in the house flickered on and off. The house was dark and cold and all the hairs on the back of my neck stood to attention like soldiers. The first night I heard a scream as if someone was dying. It all went dark and I felt something touch my hand. I froze. All I could feel was wet dripping. It was blood. The ghost yelled really creepily. "We can all be together now!"

Summer Wickham-Hughes (12)
Wyvern St Edmund's, Laverstock

FBI'S MOST WANTED

A shadow at the door had me on edge. Someone had been standing there for five minutes like they were waiting for something. I decided that the best way out of the situation was to take them out, not on a date! I crept up to the door with my gun hidden behind my back, ready to strike. I carried a backpack full of money so I could just drive to a new hotel straight away. *Haaa! That felt refreshing*, I thought to myself as I sat on the sofa in my new hotel. Then a shadow at the door...

Grace Peter (14)
Wyvern St Edmund's, Laverstock

UNEXPECTED MURDER

It had happened 1,000 times before. But this time it was different. He had a wife and a baby. People say the dead can't talk yet it told a story... It showed a shadow at the door. A shadow of a man with a sharp blade and a baby in a cot. He heard it cry but the shadowy man still held up the knife... The husband wanted to look away but couldn't. The ghostly form forcibly stabbed the baby... Then the shadows vanished. The husband looked at his hands. They were blood-soaked. What had he done?

Finn McCormack (12)
Wyvern St Edmund's, Laverstock

THE GIRL AND THE MIRROR

The tired girl had been sleeping very quietly but she woke up to a very creepy sound of banging so she ignored it and went back to bed but suddenly she noticed a girl with wavy black hair standing in her hallway. She jumped out of bed and rushed to the bathroom and splashed cold water onto her frozen face so she could forget about it. When she looked at her mirror she didn't see herself, she saw the girl in the hallway. She jumped into bed and tried to forget about the mirror and the girl.

Poppy Durham (12)
Wyvern St Edmund's, Laverstock

THE FOREVER CIRCUS

Just over a century ago a circus came to town and lots of people went and they gave them stamps. As they entered the big tent they saw all the acts. The clowns, lions and trapeze acts. Some people's stamps didn't come off that night so they went the next night and the ringleader took them to the back where everything was and showed them a room. He looked into all their souls until they were under his spell. They all became part of the act and they would live forever in the circus.

Amelia Wells (14)
Wyvern St Edmund's, Laverstock

BLOODED MURDER

Adam was walking home from work when suddenly he noticed a trail of blood. He followed the blood trail. It led him to a small dark alleyway. In the darkness he could hear a moan, he turned on the brightness of his phone, there on the floor lay a man gasping for air. Rushing over, Adam tried to keep him alive but the man took one final breath and was gone. Adam sat in a pile of blood, still trying to revive the man but it was too late. Adam knew he was not alone, he felt someone watching...

Lekeisha Eletu (13)
Wyvern St Edmund's, Laverstock

WHAT'S HAPPENING TO OUR WORLD?

It was a strange night, the street lights had been lit, but the sun was still out. I was tucked up in my bed slowly drifting to sleep. Suddenly there was a crash outside, I looked out my window. My eyes widened but there was nothing there. Out of nowhere green lightning struck. The wind whistled, trees went crumbling to the ground. What was happening? The room started to shake, the walls started to crack. That night all that was left of the house was a brick with blood trickling down it.

Lilli Clements-Champion (11)
Wyvern St Edmund's, Laverstock

WHO DID IT?

It just didn't add up... My dad was murdered. We had two suspects. His friend said they had a fight that night and he banged his head so hard it must have killed him. The next suspect was his ex-wife. Apparently, she poisoned him since she'd had a restraining order against him for a year. But my dad never liked her. The detective didn't believe either of them. My dad had no marks on his head and no poison in his blood... There was only one person it could possibly have been...

Bronte Pearce (12)
Wyvern St Edmund's, Laverstock

IF I WERE A CLUE...

The cold wind whipped around my feet as the sun rose up in the sky. *If I were a clue where would I hide?* said my mind over and over again. Then I noticed a name on a gravestone that I knew. "Vernon," I said under my breath. Suddenly a hand grabbed my ankle. I pulled away fast to reveal nothing was there.

I got the lab to run some tests on the body. "Victoria Vernon, fourteen years old, died two years ago." There was a pause then, "She also has your DNA on her left hand..."

Amelia Johns (12)
Wyvern St Edmund's, Laverstock

THE NIGHTMARE

It was very windy, very dark. A strange-looking man was staring at me. As I lifted my head and my eyes were opposite his, he died. I woke up shaking, I was out of breath after I saw that nightmare. In my head, I had a feeling that I shouldn't worry, it was only a nightmare. I got out of my bed and went to the living room. My dad was watching television, it was the news. It had the picture of a man in the dream, he was murdered by someone. Suddenly blood filled my shivering hands...

Raneem Al Slamat (12)
Wyvern St Edmund's, Laverstock

UNSOLVED

Once there was an old wooden house in a deep, dark forest. There were spiderwebs everywhere but when I set foot in the scary house there was a figure standing there and as soon as I went towards the figure it came running at me. I screamed and I was never heard of again. I just hope no one finds this house because if you go in you never come out. A few years later another person went inside the house but this time it was a child. She was only nine but the monster liked her...

Amelia Moore (13)
Wyvern St Edmund's, Laverstock

THE DEMON INSIDE

You do not know who I am but I know you. I'm assigned to you at birth, some people are meant for greatness, you I'm afraid aren't. There's no need for me to introduce my brother's fear and shame but allow me to introduce myself. I am the worst of your demons but you see me as your friend, you turn to me when you have nothing else because I live in your heart. I'm the one who forces you to endure, the one who prolongs your torment and kills you inside. Sincerely Hope. Sleep well.

Freyda Nguyen-Vincent (13)
Wyvern St Edmund's, Laverstock

GHOST SUSPECT

The suspect was gone... I left him for a minute and he vanished. I rushed out of the station to find a car missing. I remembered its plate though: 'SP35 9XL'. I typed it into my phone to find the location of the car. I rushed to my own car, and get strapped in, push the gears and pedal to the metal. He was speeding two miles ahead of me, so fast his tyre popped. A good time to pull over. My car slid over to it and the window fell slowly, only to find... no one in there at all...

Thomas James (13)
Wyvern St Edmund's, Laverstock

GUILTY BUT INNOCENT

I always hate thinking of the night when the police arrested me. I was only killing the person who killed me. It's not my fault I killed her... My best friend. I thought it was a stranger killing me. I didn't know it was a joke, didn't know it was my friend. I went to court and they told me... "She's guilty!" I knew I was innocent, but that's the story of why I am here in this tiny, empty cell. I always ask myself when I can go do it again. I enjoyed it. But I won't get caught!

Pippa-Mae Muirhead (11)

Wyvern St Edmund's, Laverstock

GUILTY

All I wanted to do was get out of that house. Those people, those memories... but I always came back. This time was different. I woke up from daydreaming as I heard a door slam. The lie detector results were back. I sat nervously in the courtroom waiting, a man opened the door and walked to the judge. "Guilty of murder!"
I pleaded I wasn't guilty as they took me away. As I sat in prison on a small hard bed a smile came over my face. Finally, I was out of that house!

Lizzie Bulpitt (14)
Wyvern St Edmund's, Laverstock

MY STORY OF PARANORMAL ACTIVITY

Many people have seen some unexplainable things. I am one of them. I was drying my hair as I'd just washed it over the side of the bathtub. My head was facing downwards and as I was moving it back up, from the side of my eye I could see a black, unidentified creature. I got up. My eyes widened. What I could see was no creature at all but a figure of a tall man looking down on me. My heart started pounding faster as I freaked out and with a blink of an eye, he was gone...

Cassie Pearce (14)
Wyvern St Edmund's, Laverstock

THE PERFECT CURE

A shadow at the door and the tapping of someone's feet had alerted me to his location, and in a flash, I had found him. He was cornered in an office when I found him, and as I approached him, I said calmly, "You have nothing to fear, you will be just fine."

With a swift step and a flash, the man was cured. The man's head smiled as it rolled off his neck, as the blood rushed up and out of where his head should have been. This man was 'cured', and he wasn't the last.

Bayley-James Jones (13)
Wyvern St Edmund's, Laverstock

THE DEAD ARE LOUDER THAN THE LIVING

People say the dead can't talk. People say ghosts aren't real. People are wrong. I know this because I can see them, and I know I cannot be the only one, not again. I guess people don't want to believe in something they can't see. But I can, I can see, and that's why I'm locking up my house. I can't let them in. If the dead know I can see, they will kill me. I look through my window and see a pale figure. They stop and look into my eyes. But it's not a stranger, it's me.

Abigail Hallen (13)
Wyvern St Edmund's, Laverstock

THE MIRROR

Sometimes I miss my deceased brother. Although I never really made an effort to get to know him. He always got home late after being at his friend's house. So after the incident, I didn't really care. When I looked in the mirror, I saw him glaring back at me, fear in his eyes. But he was dead, I saw it happen. In the end I was caught. I was sloppy, I didn't cover it up properly. So here is my letter to say I watched him suffer. I made him suffer, he deserved to suffer.

Katie Dixon (13)
Wyvern St Edmund's, Laverstock

THE MURDER

In the dead of night a news reporter found a hollowed-out body in an old shack in the middle of Aintsbury Forest. Soon after the murder a detective came to the crime scene and saw the disturbing hollowed-out corpse lying lifeless in the corner of the room. The detective went outside to check for any more evidence. The detective found some bins and opened them. Inside was another corpse with a knife but the corpse came to life and, sadly choked the detective to death...

Reuben Bowler (12)
Wyvern St Edmund's, Laverstock

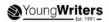

THE WISH

A little girl was having an argument with her parents about buying a new toy but they said no, she got very angry and said, "I wish you were dead!" She ran upstairs and went to bed. She had a dream that her mum and dad were about to go out when a car ran them over. She woke up crying and sprinted down the stairs. She just wanted to say sorry, just to have a hug. A lingering smell was in the air. She walked into the kitchen and looked down to see her dead parents...

Zach Hiscott (12)
Wyvern St Edmund's, Laverstock

CARTER LAKE

Nobody knew why there was a strange girl in a white nightdress found floating dead on muddy Carter Lake. Nobody knew why I was the only one who heard the scream of a girl muffled in the howling storm. And nobody knew why at 2am I could see a pale girl in a white nightdress gliding along the murky lake. All anybody knew was that people from the town of Carter had been disappearing one by one. And worst of all, all the evidence was pointing to me! Had I been framed?

Olivia Taylor (12)
Wyvern St Edmund's, Laverstock

THE DARK SHADOW MAN

Police are on a hunt for the 'Shadow Man'. A kid called Callum is watching Netflix and all of a sudden the power goes out and he can't see anything. His life flashes at the beat of his heart. A light flicks, a figure comes out. It happens again but he feels a pain in his toe. He looks down, nothing's there but his skin is coming off like a banana. He screams but it's back again and there's a gunshot. He tries to escape but he's in the forest. He can't get out.

Zara Watson (12)
Wyvern St Edmund's, Laverstock

I HATE MY JOB

I hate my job. I hate the way I make people feel. I take people, steal them from their beds, sometimes from hospitals, sometimes from the streets. People hate me, some people wish to see me, but overall the families despise me most. I leave them in sorrow and denial. I hate it, I wish I had a different job. I hate being hated. I hate taking them from the people they love. It's not my fault. I hate my job... for I am Death, but don't worry, I'll see you someday.

Megan Lynn (12)
Wyvern St Edmund's, Laverstock

THE BALL

Rolling down the dilapidated stairs, a dirty ball landed at my feet. A young angelic boy smiled next to me as I carefully handed him the ball. Curious, I asked him where his family was. He didn't answer. He just stood still hanging his head as the colour in his face went dull. He didn't cry, instead, the boy laughed menacingly. That's when the stairs broke loose. I realised I was talking to an executed supernatural. The lights flashed...

Amelia Mullaney (14)
Wyvern St Edmund's, Laverstock

THE BOY IN THE WET BIN

In the cold spacy room, he looked into the nothingness. He started to hear raspy old voices calling him into the endless void of death. After two years of pain, he got released into the world but the voices followed. But one night as he went to bed, as usual, he saw a ten-foot skinny man in a bloodstained leather suit. The last thing he remembered was the figure lurching at him. Two days later his horror-stricken mum found him in a cold wet bin.

Louis Knight (13)
Wyvern St Edmund's, Laverstock

VOICES

They say the dead can't talk. I think they can. I took my seat in the courtroom, the harsh lights making my pale skin glow. I saw him in the corner. He was given a life sentence. I knew he could hear me, whispering guilt into his head. I knew no one else could. If you think the dead can't talk; you're probably okay. But if you've ever heard disembodied voices calling to you from the shadows; you're in trouble. Big trouble...

Catherine Hinder (14)
Wyvern St Edmund's, Laverstock

A KIDNAP

She was only five... His shadow lurked in the hallway like a leopard waiting to pounce. A thick sense of evil drifted around the house, every step he took. A dense coat of dust majestically sprinkled from the ceiling as he crept. A silhouette in the doorway stood and two beaming eyes reflected off the glowing moon. He stepped over to the bed and placed his hand gently on the bed... He picked her up and left. She was only five.

Casey Mullen (14)
Wyvern St Edmund's, Laverstock

RIGHT IN FRONT OF ME

Once there was a woman, who was a bounty hunter, calling a bunch of shops and businesses asking if they had seen the man they were looking for. She eventually got tired and decided to get up and grab a coffee from the office. While she was pouring the milk her boss walked in. "I have your new partner in crime Saffron, his name is Michael. Michael say hi to Saffron." Saffron's mouth fell to the floor as well as her coffee.

Ruby Goddard (12)
Wyvern St Edmund's, Laverstock

THE NEIGHBOURS UPSTAIRS

I woke up jolting upright, I could have sworn I heard a thud sound from upstairs. I knew my neighbours were loud but this wasn't their usual yelling match. I didn't know what to do so I went out to check... The door was wide open. I took a few steps in and I saw them sprawled out on the floor, lifeless. They were long gone when the doctors got there. "So," the detective paused, "so is this the truth or was it you?"

George Chapman (12)
Wyvern St Edmund's, Laverstock

BORN A PSYCHOPATH

Tension building, silence crammed in the lonely interrogation room. There sits a middle-aged woman and undercover police. Questions being thrown left to right convincing the truth to spill. All emotions were shown by the mysterious woman. Only for her to know, they were fake. The report filled with lies. Voices in her mind have no remorse for what she committed. But yet to be discovered. Born to be a psychopath!

Keira Crossen (14)
Wyvern St Edmund's, Laverstock

KILLER

I am a murderer. I injected insulin underneath his tongue so the doctors would think he was an undiagnosed diabetic, he had a heart attack shortly after the insulin was in him. I dug a 10ft hole in a nearby forest and threw him in. I put some dirt on him then chucked a dead animal on top so the police would think the smell and blood was from a dead animal. I killed my husband.

Daisy Barney (14)
Wyvern St Edmund's, Laverstock

MURDER AT THE BUS STOP

I observed it happen. The murder of Matilda Richman. She was at the bus stop. A person strode up behind her, it was the police's most wanted fugitive. Then I heard a splat! Her blood ran down the bus shelter. She tumbled down and then he situated a rose on her.

I turned around and called 911. I turned around once again. He was gone. The police arrived a minute later.

Matthew Osgood (12)
Wyvern St Edmund's, Laverstock

THE PAST

People think the dead can't talk. These people are wrong. I read the threatening words yet again that lay on my bed. I know who they are from... A few years ago, my husband went missing and I have lived alone ever since. It was a Thursday night. I went to bed, but there was no note... Nothing. Voices filled in my house with whispers. My past was coming to haunt me.

Sophie Everett (14)
Wyvern St Edmund's, Laverstock

POLICE INSPECTOR

An inspector woke up in the middle of the night upset about not finding the murder weapon from the murderer. He went into his drawer to get a bottle of water. He found the murder weapon with stained blood on it! He threw it out of his window. Later when he cautiously pulled his drawer open there it was again, the bloodstained murder weapon!

Alexia Roxburgh (12)
Wyvern St Edmund's, Laverstock

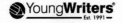

YOUNG WRITERS
INFORMATION

We hope you have enjoyed reading this book – and
that you will continue to in the coming years.

If you're a young writer who enjoys reading and creative
writing, or the parent of an enthusiastic poet or story writer,
visit our website **www.youngwriters.co.uk/subscribe** to join
the World of Young Writers and receive news, competitions,
writing challenges, tips, articles and giveaways! There
is lots to keep budding writers motivated to write!

If you would like to order further copies of this book,
or any of our other titles, then please give us a
call or order via your online account.

Young Writers
Remus House
Coltsfoot Drive
Peterborough
PE2 9BF
(01733) 890066
info@youngwriters.co.uk

Join in the conversation!
Tips, news, giveaways and much more!

 YoungWritersUK   @YoungWritersCW   YoungWritersCW